DONNA GRANT'S
best-selling romance novels

"Time travel, ancient legends, and seductive romance are seamlessly interwoven into one captivating package."
—Publishers Weekly on Midnight's Master

"Dark, sexy, magical. When I want to indulge in a sizzling fantasy adventure, I read Donna Grant."
—Allison Brennan, *New York Times* bestseller

5 Stars! Top Pick! "An absolute must read! From beginning to end, it's an incredible ride."
—Night Owl Reviews

"It's good vs. evil Druid in the next installment of Grant's Dark Warrior series. The stakes get higher as discerning one's true loyalties become harder. Grant's compelling characters and continued presence of previous protagonists are key reasons why these books are so gripping. Another exciting and thrilling chapter!"
—RT Book Reviews on Midnight's Lover

"I definitely recommend Dangerous Highlander, even to skeptics of paranormal romance – you just may fall in love with the MacLeods."
—The Romance Reader

Don't miss these other spellbinding novels by
DONNA GRANT

CHIASSON SERIES
Wild Fever
Wild Dream

DARK KING SERIES
Dark Heat
Darkest Flame
Fire Rising
Burning Desire

DARK WARRIOR SERIES
Midnight's Master
Midnight's Lover
Midnight's Seduction
Midnight's Warrior
Midnight's Kiss
Midnight's Captive
Midnight's Temptation
Midnight's Promise
Midnight's Surrender

DARK SWORD SERIES
Dangerous Highlander
Forbidden Highlander
Wicked Highlander
Untamed Highlander
Shadow Highlander
Darkest Highlander

ROGUES OF SCOTLAND SERIES
The Craving

SHIELD SERIES

A Dark Guardian
A Kind of Magic
A Dark Seduction
A Forbidden Temptation
A Warrior's Heart

DRUIDS GLEN SERIES

Highland Mist
Highland Nights
Highland Dawn
Highland Fires
Highland Magic
Dragonfyre

SISTERS OF MAGIC TRILOGY

Shadow Magic
Echoes of Magic
Dangerous Magic

Royal Chronicles Novella Series

Prince of Desire
Prince of Seduction
Prince of Love
Prince of Passion

Wicked Treasures Novella Series

Seized by Passion
Enticed by Ecstasy
Captured by Desire

**And look for more anticipated novels from
Donna Grant**

Fire Rising (Dark Kings)
Masters of Seduction
Wild Need – (Chiasson)

coming soon!

WILD DREAM

A Chiasson Story

Donna Grant

WILD DREAM

© 2014 by DL Grant, LLC
Excerpt from *Fire Rising* copyright © 2014 by Donna Grant

Cover design © 2013 by Leah Suttle

ISBN 10: 0991454235
ISBN 13: 978-0991454235

www.DonnaGrant.com

Available in ebook and print editions

ACKNOWLEDGEMENTS

A special thanks goes out to my family who lives in the bayous of Louisiana. Those summers I spent there are some of my most precious memories. I also need to send a shout-out to my team – Melissa Bradley, Stephanie Dalvit, and Leah Suttle. You guys are the bomb. Seriously. Hats off to my editor, Chelle Olson, and cover design extraordinaire, Leah Suttle. Thank you all for helping me get this story out!

Steve, Gillian, and Connor, thanks for putting up with my hectic schedule and for knowing when it was time that I got out of the house. And a special hug for my furbabies Lexi, Sheba, Sassy, Tinkerbell, and Diego who always demand some loving regardless of what I'm doing.

Last but not least, my readers. You have my eternal gratitude for the amazing support you show me and my books. Y'all rock my world. Stay tuned at the end of this story for the first sneak peek of *Fire Rising*, Dark Kings book 2 out June 3, 2014. Enjoy!

Xoxo
Donna

CHAPTER ONE

Lafayette Regional Airport
July

Ava Ledet stepped off the private jet and smiled when her gaze landed on Olivia Breaux. Olivia's dark hair was pulled back in a ponytail, and her black eyes crinkled at the corners as she smiled. She pushed off the truck she had been leaning against and ran to Ava.

"I can't believe you're finally here," Olivia said as she enveloped Ava in a hug.

Ava wasn't a touchy-feely type person, but Olivia never gave her a choice. In the short time they had worked together, Ava felt as if she had found her first true friend.

She returned Olivia's hug, genuinely happy to see her. "I'm sorry I'm so late."

Olivia stepped back and raised her brow at the private jet. "Flying in style though, aren't you?"

"Company jet. They allow us to use it every now and again."

"Your law firm must really bring in the big bucks."

Ava didn't respond to the comment. Instead, she turned to the co-pilot who held out her bag. "Thanks, Jim."

Jim gave her a wink and entered the plane. Olivia hooked her arm with Ava's while turning her to the truck.

Olivia leaned in and whispered, "He's cute."

"I suppose." She glanced over her shoulder to see Jim's tall form bend to enter the plane. He looked at her, his hazel eyes holding hers a moment before he closed the door and disappeared.

"You suppose," Olivia repeated in surprise. "Ava, he's a hunk."

Ava grinned and opened the door to the truck where she tossed her bag. "All right. I admit it. I'm not blind. I've seen his cute ass. But I'm not looking for a guy. I'm too busy with work to even dream about going on a date, much less actually going on said date."

Not to mention there was her past, the same past she had returned to Louisiana to face.

When Olivia didn't respond, Ava looked up to see her black eyes watching her thoughtfully. Ava had seen that look before, though not from Olivia. It had come from her mother.

Ava got into the passenger seat and strapped on her seat belt. Just being in Louisiana was more difficult than she had expected, but she could handle it. She had made a name for herself in Dallas as one of the best attorneys in the city. If she could handle courtrooms, juries, and judges, she could handle the part of her life that had nearly ruined everything.

Olivia cleared her throat as she climbed into the truck. "It's not that far of a drive, but I'm starving, and the boys will only wait so long before they dive into the food."

Ava laughed, grateful that Olivia talked of something so mundane. She looked around the interior of the Chevy truck. "The last time I saw you, you were driving a car. Is this yours?"

"Yep." Olivia's face scrunched as she drove away from the airfield. "I was in a bit of an accident and needed a new vehicle. In this area, it's better to have a truck."

Ava looked at Olivia to see an aura of happiness about her that hadn't been there before. "You've changed. I guess we can say that your man has something to do with that."

Even though Ava had gotten the lawsuit against Olivia dismissed the month before, they still talked often. It hadn't taken Olivia long to spill the beans on Vincent, the man who had swept her off her feet. Ava was happy for her friend. In her world, all she ever heard of were divorces. It was nice to see that love did exist.

For some.

"Yes," Olivia said dreamily. "Vin is...well, he's amazing."

"He has to have one flaw."

Olivia merely smiled and cut her eyes to Ava.

Ava laughed. "I really want to meet him now."

"How long has it been since you've been to Louisiana?" Olivia asked.

The smile dropped from Ava's face, and she hastily looked out her window so Olivia wouldn't see. "It seems a lifetime ago. I was thirteen when we left. The day after Christmas."

"Fourteen years? That is a long time."

Ava stared out the window, but it wasn't the rice fields she saw. It was a flood of memories from a happier time – a time before her world was ripped apart.

"Are you all right?"

Ava roughly shoved aside the hated memories, and threw a smile at Olivia. "Of course."

Olivia's frown remained in place. "For a lawyer, you're a terrible liar."

"Why did the party get moved from your grandmother's?" she asked, hoping Olivia would let her change the subject. The one thing Ava never did was talk about her past.

Olivia paused as she turned off the paved road. "Maman loves to cook for people, but Vin convinced her to use his kitchen. It's easily twice the size of Maman's. Needless to say, he only had to say that once before she jumped at the chance to use it."

It was only a little later that the truck turned onto a drive lined by massive live oak trees dripping with thick moss. Through the trees, there were clusters of crepe myrtles drenched in bright pink, white, red, and pale pink blooms.

"My God. This is gorgeous," Ava said as she leaned forward to get a better look at the trees.

There was a smile on Olivia's face. "Wait until you see the house."

No sooner had the words left Olivia's mouth than Ava spotted the white plantation house. She felt as if she had stepped back in time, that the busy world she knew was gone – never to be seen again. And part of her enjoyed the thought of that.

Olivia parked the truck at the side of the house behind the others and got out. Ava closed her mouth and opened the door to slide to the ground. She went to grab her bag when a large hand wrapped around the handles.

Startled, she jerked her head to the side to find a tall man with short, dark hair and a red tee that showcased every rippling muscle. He flashed her a smile, but his bright blue eyes were what arrested her.

"Thanks, Christian," Olivia said. "Christian, this is Ava Ledet. Ava, this is one of Vincent's brothers, Christian."

Christian gallantly took her hand. "Nice to finally meet you, Ava. Olivia has told us so much about you."

Ava hadn't realized until that moment how she missed the Cajun accent. She was forced to tear her gaze away from Christian when Olivia turned her around so that Ava could get a good look at the backyard. The bayou was about two hundred feet from the house. The grass was a rich green while the leaves of the live oaks and cypress trees were a darker green. The sun hung in a cloudless sky, and the water of the bayou appeared fathomless.

"Take a deep breath and prepare," Olivia whispered.

Ava glanced at her, unsure of what she meant until her gaze landed on the men under the covered deck of the house. It was almost as if she had stepped into the cover of Hunk Daily. Every man there was supremely gorgeous.

Her lungs seized when she spotted one of the men, beer in hand, leaning casually against a thick post next to the grill. He had long, dark hair that fell to his shoulders. The top half was pulled away from his face and held at the back of his head with a leather strap.

His white V-neck tee molded to his muscular body and wide shoulders, and his dark denim jeans hung low on trim hips. As spectacular as his body was, it was his face that kept drawing her gaze.

He had a square jaw and chin with dark brows that slashed over his eyes. She was too far away to see his eyes, but she had a suspicion they were brilliant blue. His lips were wide and inviting. He smiled easily, making the corners of his eyes crinkle.

In a word, he was striking.

Before Ava could mentally get her feet underneath her, she and Olivia reached the deck. That's when she noticed the many fans that hung from the ceiling and kept the air moving and the occupants cool.

The man at the barreled grill closed the lid and smiled seductively at Olivia before he walked to her. Ava couldn't help but smile while she watched Vincent pull Olivia into his arms and kiss her languidly.

Ava looked away, and found her gaze snagged by the intense blue eyes of the man she had been drooling over just seconds before. They stared at each other for several moments. She was drawn to him, like an invisible string connected them and tugged her to him.

He didn't push away from the post and walk to greet her, and Ava was both glad and perturbed that he didn't. She wanted to know his name, wanted to get a closer look at his face. Then she reminded herself that she hadn't come to Louisiana to find a man. She had come because she wanted to see Olivia, but also because she had something to do.

There was no time for a dalliance of *any* kind.

It was really too bad. Whoever the man was, he left her breathless, unbalanced.

Lustful.

Perspiration dampened her skin, and it had nothing to do with the heat. Her mouth was dry, and she throbbed low in her stomach. If he could do that with just a look, what would he do to her with a kiss? Or...more? Part of Ava desperately wanted to find out.

"Vincent Chiasson, don't you let that meat burn," a petite woman with silver hair pulled back in a bun chastised from the door of the back porch.

She wiped her hands on her apron as she smiled at Olivia. "Sha, you're back. And you must be Ava. My, aren't you a pretty one."

"Maman, Vincent knows what he's doing," Olivia said, even as Vincent hurried back to the grill.

Ava's ears were filled with a rushing noise as black dots edged her vision. Chiasson. Olivia's grandmother had said Chiasson. It couldn't be possible.

"Ava?" Olivia said and touched her arm.

She swallowed and took a step to the side. *Breathe. Just open your lungs and breathe, dammit.* "I'm fine."

"It's the heat," Maria said. "Get her inside to cool off."

Suddenly, a bottle of beer was shoved in her hands. "This should do the trick," Christian said and walked her to a chair under one of the fans.

Olivia pulled a chair next to her and peered at her closely. "You look as pale as death."

She felt it as well. How did she not know Vincent's last name was Chiasson? Hadn't it come up in conversations with Olivia? No. She would have remembered, because that name was burned, no, seared into her memory.

"I'm fine." Ava forced the words past her lips and lifted the beer to her mouth. She hated beer, but right now an adult beverage was an adult beverage. And she needed a lot of alcohol. An entire store still wouldn't take the edge off.

Olivia blew out a breath. "All right. Then let me

make the introductions. You already met Christian. The hunk who kissed me is Vincent."

Ava looked toward the grill to find Vincent smiling at them. She gave a nod of her head.

"Next up is Lincoln, the brooding one next to my man."

So the hunk had a name. Lincoln. His blue eyes were the exact color as both Christian's and Vincent's. Ava once more found herself ensnared in his gaze. Lincoln lifted his beer in a salute to her and promptly turned away to answer his cell phone.

"The lazy bum in the hammock is Beau. Normally he's in the kitchen. He's an amazing cook, but Maman promptly shooed him out this morning," Olivia said with a laugh.

Beau lifted his head long enough for Ava to see the same vivid blue eyes that the rest of the Chiasson clan had. His hair wasn't nearly as long as Vincent's and Lincoln's, but the semi-long length looked good on him. "Nice to have you here, Ava."

The entire scene was surreal. It was bad enough that she was back in Louisiana, but she was also just down the road from where she grew up. To make the situation even more bizarre, she was in the Chiasson home. As a guest.

There was no way she could pull off what she wanted to do. It was all too much. All around her were the sounds of the bayou, the smell of nature at its finest. At one time, it had been her life's blood.

The Cajun accent of the people, the sounds of Zydeco music playing in the background, the smell of spices from the food. It brought a deluge of memories back that threatened to drown her.

Somehow, she got through the next thirty minutes as Vincent finished cooking the meat. Ava plastered a smile on her face as they all sat around the table outside that was laden with food made by Maria. She ate the delicious meal and savored every bite.

Because she knew the idealistic scene was about to be shattered.

CHAPTER TWO

Lincoln wanted to forget the haunting beauty that was Ava Ledet, with her long, wavy auburn hair and unusual amber eyes. She walked fluidly, almost as if she glided upon air.

She had the look of a city girl, but there was something in the way that she gazed longingly at the bayou. Then there was her creamy skin, only accentuated by the black shirt that molded to her pert breasts. And, of course, her tight white pants.

Lincoln watched her help Olivia clear the table, and bit back a moan as she bent over and he got a view of her breasts when her collar dipped.

"She's very pretty," Beau said as he walked up and handed Lincoln a beer.

"Yep."

Pretty was like calling the Grand Canyon a hole in the ground. Ava was...enthralling, spellbinding.

Captivating.

She was calm and easy-going now, but he would wager his best knives that she had a temper to go with that hair of hers. Her face was that of an angel, with her high cheekbones and wide, expressive eyes. But her sensual mouth and tempting curves hinted at a sexier side that Lincoln itched to bring out of her.

"Are you laying claim, because I'm definitely interested," Beau said.

Lincoln paused with his beer half way to his lips, and slanted a glare at his youngest brother.

Beau chuckled and shook his head. "I get the point, Linc. Stop with the look. By the way, who called earlier? You looked upset."

Shit. How could he have forgotten about Solomon's call? As his gaze once more snagged on Ava, he knew exactly why he had forgotten.

"Is it bad?" Beau asked.

"Bad enough. I can't exactly tell the family with Ava here."

Beau rubbed his jaw. "Christian brought her bag into the house. Is she staying?"

"I hope to hell not." For several reasons. The main one being that Lincoln didn't think he could keep his distance from her.

Beau nudged him with his elbow. "You need to tell Vin that."

Lincoln waited for Olivia to take Ava down to the water before he made his way to the house. Maria was sitting on the porch as he walked up.

"A fine meal, Maria. Thank you."

She smiled, a knowing look in her dark eyes. "Don't think I didn't see you looking at Ava as if she were the finest dessert served up on a platter just for you. She was looking at you as well, boo."

Lincoln didn't even try to lie to the old woman. She might not be family yet, but he had known Maria since his birth. After their parents' deaths, she had looked out for all five of the Chiasson children — or as much as they would let her — despite raising her own granddaughter.

"Ava's a looker, but she's just visiting."

"For now," Maria said shrewdly. "You don't know what the future holds, Linc. Remember that."

"Yes, ma'am." He had a grin on his face when he walked into the house that lasted until he reached the office doorway. He didn't have to search to know that Vin was in the office.

Lincoln walked straight into the office and found Vincent writing in the family journal that listed all the paranormal beings the family had killed throughout the years, and how to kill them.

Vincent looked up and stopped writing. "What is it?"

"I got a call from New Orleans."

That was all that needed to be said for Vin to lay down his pen. "Get the others."

"Ava is here."

A muscle twitched in Vincent's jaw. "It's that bad?"

"I don't think you'll want to be explaining things to her."

"No, no. You're right. We'll have to wait until

Olivia, Maria, and Ava return to Maria's." Vincent ran a hand down his face. "Olivia won't be happy about being kept in the dark."

Lincoln turned on his heel and quickly found Beau and Christian in the kitchen. The three walked back to the office to join Vin. Beau lounged on the loveseat while Christian sat on the edge of the chair, his elbows on his knees.

Lincoln leaned a hip on the edge of the desk so he could see everyone. "I received a call from New Orleans. There's a bit of a problem that they've asked for our help with."

"We never turn family away," Vincent said.

Christian laced his fingers together. "They're cousins. It's a no brainer. When do we go?"

"We don't." Lincoln set down his beer. "Solomon said that Kane is on his way here."

Beau jerked into a sitting position. "The next full moon is a day away. What the hell is Kane doing traveling now?"

"It seems our cousin doesn't know how not to piss off a Voodoo priestess."

Vincent let out a long sign. "Not again."

"We can't handle this with Ava here."

"Afraid I'll learn your Chiasson secrets?" Ava's voice said from behind him.

Lincoln stilled, her voice going through him like a blade. He slowly straightened and moved to the wall so he could see the doorway. And her. Ava and Olivia stood in the entry of the double doors no one had thought to close.

There had been something in Ava's voice,

almost a hint of fury.

"I was coming to tell you that we're headed to Maman's," Olivia told Vincent.

Vin stood and leaned his hands on the desk. "Ava, please forgive us. There is some family business that we like to keep private."

"You mean how your family hunts the supernatural?" she said offhandedly. "I used to live in this area. I know about the Chiasson family."

There was more to her story. Lincoln was sure of it. And he wanted to know what it was. "Olivia said you left as a child. I doubt you knew very much."

Her amber gaze swung to him. Her smile was cold and laced with such anger that her eyes burned with it. "When I was twelve, my father lost his half-brother in an accident. At least that's what the papers called it. My father suspected something else, so he began to look into it. For the next six months, he researched the paranormal. Ultimately, it led him to the Chiassons."

"Oh, God," Olivia whispered, her eyes wide as she stared at Ava. "That's why you looked faint when you learned the family name."

Lincoln's mind raced with the people his parents had brought into the house, trying to place Ava's father.

"My father began hunting the creatures. It became his obsession. He quit his job, would sleep all day, but the worst was when he left. He walked out on his wife and daughter. To hunt the supernatural."

"Jack," Lincoln said as he finally remembered. "Jack Ledet was your father."

Lincoln recalled how much Jack had spoken of his family. He was obsessed with killing the supernatural – but to protect his wife and daughter. There was no way he would have just walked out on them. Lincoln may have only been in his early teens, but his father had taught them all to recognize a good man when they saw one. Jack was a good man.

"Where is he?" Ava asked.

Lincoln frowned and looked at Vin. Vin shrugged his shoulders.

"We've not seen Jack in years," Vincent said. "We assumed he returned home and was finished with hunting."

"Assumed." Ava pinned him with a withering look. "Did it not occur to any of you that one of those *creatures* might have gotten him?"

Lincoln shook his head and stepped forward so that Ava would look at him. "The last time we saw Jack was years ago. We finished a hunt, and he shared breakfast with us before he started back home. We all thought he finally had enough of the life."

He wanted to help Ava locate Jack, but he couldn't do anything until the full moon had passed, and Kane had gotten out of his mess.

"I'll take Ava and Maman home now," Olivia said.

Lincoln didn't want Ava to go, but by the look on her face, she needed to get away from the

Chiassons. Vincent walked Olivia out, and Lincoln found himself standing at the door watching them get into the truck and drive away.

Vincent walked back into the house and closed the door. He let out a long sigh as all four brothers stood in the large foyer. "Well, that was a surprise."

"I feel sorry for her," Christian said.

Beau swirled the last bit of his beer in the bottle. "It seems we've got two issues to deal with now. I want to help Ava find her father. I was pretty young, but I remember Jack."

Christian nodded. "Riley used to sit on his lap."

Lincoln missed his sister, but as the youngest of the clan – and the only girl – Riley deserved something more than the Chiasson family business, which was why she was in Austin at the University of Texas.

"One thing at a time," Vincent stated. "First, lets get this business with Kane sorted out. What does Solomon want us to do?"

"What do you think with a full moon coming?" Lincoln said testily.

Christian walked away toward the kitchen. "If we're going to argue, I need to get fortified with some of that chocolate cake Maria made."

Beau made a dash through the dining room to beat Christian to it, while Vincent and Lincoln leisurely walked to the kitchen. When they reached it, both Beau and Christian had a piece of cake in hand, eating.

Lincoln pulled one of the chairs at the table out and turned it around so that he straddled it, his arms resting on the back. "The Voodoo priestess has altered Kane's curse. He'll forget he's really human while in wolf form. He'll kill indiscriminately."

"He really fucked up this time," Beau said.

Vincent remained standing and began to pace. "Will the cage we have hold him?"

"If he gets here in time," Lincoln answered. "That was another of Solomon's worries. There were those trying to prevent Kane from leaving New Orleans. Solomon, Myles, and Court got him out, but they don't think it'll stop there. The people know he's coming to us."

A horrified expression crossed Christian's face as he swallowed the last of his cake. "Why would they want to keep Kane in New Orleans?"

"To punish him," Vincent said. He stopped and heaved out a breath.

Lincoln nodded. "Vin is right. He'll see what he's done when the dawn comes. It's likely to destroy him."

"What did Kane do to be punished so severely?" Beau asked.

"Solomon didn't provide that information, and I didn't ask. I figure Kane will tell us the entire tale when he gets here."

"If he gets here," Vincent said.

Lincoln glanced at his watch. "Solomon called two hours ago. It takes three to get here by car from New Orleans, but Kane is on foot. He'll come through the bayous and stay off main highways since he's being followed."

"We need to get ready then. Kane could arrive at any time," Christian said.

Vin rested his hands on the back of a chair. "I've got a bad feeling that he won't get here until tomorrow night. When he's already shifted. Before we can get him into the cage."

"That means we'll need to be on patrol starting tonight," Beau said. "We alert everyone we can. Those we can't, we keep an eye on."

Vincent and Beau filed out of the kitchen. Lincoln stood and pushed the chair under the table. He turned and found Christian blocking his way.

"We're going to need you fully in this."

Lincoln frowned and crossed his arms over his chest. "When have I ever *not* been fully involved?"

"Never. Then again, Ava Ledet didn't walk into your life until today. The others may not see it, but I do, Linc."

"See what exactly?" He thought he'd been doing a hell of a job keeping his desire hidden.

Christian raised a dark brow. "Your desire to protect her. That could get her – and you – killed."

"Not going to happen."

"Focus on her once Kane is in the cage. Until then, do us all a favor and forget her."

If only it were that easy.

CHAPTER THREE

Ava was so lost in her memories of the night her father left and never returned that she didn't realize they had reached their destination until Maria patted her on the shoulder.

"Come inside, sha," she said and exited out of the back passenger door.

Ava got out of the truck and grabbed her bag. She closed the door and sighed before she turned and faced Olivia. "If I'd have known it was the Chiassons you were involved with, I wouldn't have come."

"Then it's a good thing it never got brought up before today." Olivia smiled softly. "You have every right to your anger, but I don't believe you're mad at Vincent or any of the other Chiassons."

"I'm angry at what they did that lured my father away. I'm furious that he got involved with the hunting, and I'm sad that his half-brother was killed by something so awful. But you're right. It's my father I'm really irate at. He left us."

"You don't know that for sure," Olivia pointed out. "You heard the guys. Your father was always talking about you and your mother. The hunting he did was to keep you safe. A man like that doesn't walk out on his family."

"Then where has he been the last fourteen years?" Ava was so tired of wondering that.

Olivia took Ava's bag and wrapped an arm around her shoulders while leading her to the house. "Hopefully we'll find out. It's why you really came, isn't it?"

Ava nodded and looked at the white house. They walked around to the side where she spotted a long dock that went all the way out to the bayou. Like most other houses in the area, it had a screened in porch that overlooked the water.

They climbed the steps, walked through the porch, and into the quaint house. Maria made use of every inch of space, but the house had a relaxed feel.

Ava felt right at home instantly. It also helped that Olivia and Maria took care of her. Olivia put her bag in a back room, and Maria motioned her to one of the plush chairs in what was obviously the living room.

The house, built almost a hundred years earlier, had an open living area to optimize air flow and keep the rooms cool. Ava had no sooner taken a seat than Maria put a mug in her hands.

"It's coffee milk. It always made Olivia feel

better," she said with a wink.

Ava smiled and drank the coffee that was more milk than anything, but it did exactly what Maria wanted it to do – made her relax.

When Olivia joined them, Maria handed her a cup. All three sipped for a while before Olivia lowered her mug. "You said you and your mother remained for a year before y'all left. What happened?"

Ava remembered that night as if it happened yesterday. "It was the day after Christmas. Mom got a job anywhere she could. At one point, she worked three jobs just to pay the bills and put food on the table. Every morning I woke thinking that I would see my father. I knew the week of Christmas that something was going to happen. Mom kept counting money she had put away and boxing things up."

"She was getting ready to take you away," Maria said.

"Yes." Ava hadn't realized that at the time though. "It wasn't until the morning after Christmas that I saw the resignation on her face mixed with determination. She told me to get my stuff. She had stayed up all night packing everything away. In six hours, everything was in boxes, and we were on our way to Texas. I cried the whole way. The last bit of hope I had that my father might return disappeared somewhere on I-10 when we crossed into Texas."

"Your mother must have had her reasons for leaving. She needed a fresh start is my guess,"

Maria said.

Olivia lifted one shoulder. "I don't know. To take Jack's daughter away? What if he returned that night and had no idea where to find them?"

"That's the same thing I told Mom," Ava said. "Her response was that he had over a year to find his way home and he hadn't, which meant he didn't want us."

Maria shook her silver head and got to her feet. "That's a tough one. I'm going to Grace's for a while and leave you young girls alone. Don't get into too much trouble," she said as she grabbed her purse and walked out of the house.

Ava looked at Olivia and shared a laugh.

Olivia set aside her mug and reached for her laptop. "I've been thinking. There has to be some kind of record of your father. These days, people can't sneeze without it showing up somewhere."

Ava swallowed, suddenly overcome with emotion. "I've done a little searching on my own, but that was in Dallas. I even hired a Private Investigator for a little while."

"What did he find?"

"Nothing. That's why I came. I knew if there was even a chance for me to find my father, it was better with me in Louisiana."

"Then we'll find him," Olivia said with a reassuring smile.

After two hours of searching online and Olivia

making some calls, Ava had to get out of the house. And she knew exactly where she wanted to go.

"Can I borrow the keys to your truck?"

Olivia didn't hesitate to toss them to her. "Sure. Want me to come with you?"

"Not this time. I need to be alone for a little bit."

Olivia stood and walked with Ava to the door. "I'm not trying to be nosey, but can you tell me where you're going? I ask because I know what my man and his family hunts, and night is coming soon."

"I'm going to the house where I grew up."

"In Lafayette?"

"On the outskirts. I won't be gone long."

Olivia gave her a hug. "Keep your cell near. And call when you're on your way back."

"Will do," Ava promised and walked out of the house.

She drew in a deep breath once she was in the truck. Seeing her old house was something she had to do – no matter how painful it was.

Lincoln hid in a clump of cypress trees and surveyed the expanse of bayou around him. He was thankful it didn't get dark until well after eight. That gave them more time to search for Kane in the light.

All of their friends had been notified to remain inside for the night, and a few had even offered to help keep a lookout for Kane.

It had been years since he or his brothers had seen their family in New Orleans. That branch tended to keep to themselves, not that he blamed them. He would do the same if a Voodoo priestess had cursed their entire family to be werewolves.

Lincoln looked at the setting sun. They had another twenty minutes of good light at best before twilight hit and that eerie time between light and dark descended. Most people didn't realize that was the most dangerous time to be out.

He nudged a snapping turtle out of the way as he moved to a different location. The fading sun glinted off the eyes of a large gator resting on the banks, his gaze trained on Lincoln.

"Don't even try it," he warned the gator. "I'm after something else entirely this night, but if you push me, I'll take you home for dinner."

The problem was, none of the Chiassons could kill Kane. He was family, and on his way to them for help. It wasn't Kane's fault that he was being tracked by a relentless group determined to see him go on a killing spree.

Lincoln was of half a mind to track the fuckers, bind them together, and let Kane have at them. It's what they deserved for detaining him just so he could kill some innocent person.

His mind immediately went to Ava. He knew she was safe with Olivia. Then there was Vincent, who had set up watch near Olivia as well. Ava was more than protected. Still, Lincoln couldn't stop the knot of doubt from forming in his gut. He wanted to see her with his own eyes, to know with unwavering certainty that she was all right.

But that wasn't going to happen. He had to trust Olivia and Vincent.

Lincoln paused, the water rippling slightly around him as he spotted something moving in the brush ahead on the shoreline. He slowly withdrew both of his Bowie knives and waited.

With him on the outskirts of Crowley, he had a good chance of being the one to encounter Kane or the group after his cousin. The full moon didn't technically begin until the next night, but anyone who hunted werewolves knew that they had the day before and the day after a full moon when they would shift.

The lower the sun sank, the higher the moon rose. It was going to be tricky to get Kane in the cage before nightfall. And Lincoln couldn't rely on his brothers for help. Everyone was dispersed in a wide range for maximum opportunity in finding Kane.

But that also left them exposed. Which was going to be a complete bitch when night hit.

The bush rustled again. Lincoln tightened his grip on his knives and waited. A moment later, a raccoon ambled out and rose up on its hind legs as it chatted at him angrily. A second later it ran off.

Lincoln let out a breath and just happened to look down in time to see the water move around his legs. He spun around in time to see the gator disappear beneath the water not five feet from him.

"Fuck me," he murmured.

A second gator slid into the water off to his left. "Fuck me sideways," he hissed.

Lincoln wasted no time in getting out of the bayou. Once on land, both alligators swam away. Damn, but he hated full moons. The animals went crazy.

He looked at the sky and grimaced when he caught sight of the sunset. Everything was drenched in gold, including the water. It was a magnificent sight. It was also an omen of bad things to come.

All Lincoln could hope for, was that Kane was the only thing they would have to hunt during this full moon. If not, things were going to get hairy.

It was the quiet of the bayou, and the way sound bounced over the water, that allowed him to hear the shouts of agitation and fear. Lincoln sheathed his knives in the holsters strapped to his legs and took off running in the direction of the yells.

Lincoln dodged low hanging branches and the deepest parts of the bayous. He jumped fences, raced over private property, and took every shortcut he knew. When he scaled the last wooden fence and jumped over the side, he looked up to find Christian standing over Paul Boudreaux who was on the ground, unmoving.

"Glad you got here," Christian told him, his crossbow aimed and his eyes never leaving a large shadow in front of him.

Lincoln slowly straightened and pulled out his weapons. "Is it Kane?"

"I don't know. I arrived to find Paul right there, and spotted something large moving off. Hard to tell in this damn twilight just what it is." Christian sighed. "I think it's Kane."

"Let's hope it is. I don't want to be hunting something else as well."

Lincoln took a quick survey of the area. It was dense with tall pines and giant live oaks. Perfect hiding area for anything. It could come at them from above, or from any of the numerous shadows.

All in all, it was a sucky night.

Lincoln motioned to get his brother's attention. He pointed to Christian and told him to stay put before he pointed to himself and used his hand to tell Christian that he was going to go behind the creature. Christian gave a nod of understanding.

Lincoln carefully, silently, put one foot in front of the other and slowly walked around the large shadow. When he was behind it, he heard the unmistakable growl of a werewolf just before he leapt out of the shadow at him.

CHAPTER FOUR

Ava knew seeing her old home was going to be a bit like getting kicked in the stomach, but knowing it and experiencing it were two different things. She had pulled along the side of the road in the neighborhood, and for long minutes she merely sat in the truck staring at the house. When she lived in the house it had been painted yellow with white trim. Now the small house was a sand color with navy trim. Shutters had been added to the outside of the windows in the same navy.

That wasn't the only difference. Her mother's rose bed had been ripped up, replaced with crepe myrtle trees and day lilies. The stone path she had helped her father put down from the rock-lined drive was also gone. In its place was a concrete path that matched the concrete drive.

There were no more tears to shed. Ava had given all she had years ago, but that didn't stop the sadness from descending. Her parents had been happy there once.

The three of them had been happy once – before it all fell apart.

If she was ever going to move on with her life and shut the door to her past, she had to find her father. No matter how long it took, no matter what she had to do, she had to know where he was.

Ava sank lower in the seat when the house door opened and a young couple came out and got in their SUV. Ava waited until they drove away before she peeked her head up. She was about to start the truck when she looked at the house again. After waiting until the taillights of the SUV were out of sight, she got out of the truck and stood in the street.

The neighborhood had grown a lot in fourteen years, but that's not what she had come to see. Her feet felt stuck in concrete as she walked to the other side of the road and stood before the yard she had used to play in.

It was several minutes before she got up the nerve to step upon the grass. It was more than strange standing in the yard. She had remembered it being so much bigger. Then again, everything was big to a kid.

She smiled as she recalled her father teaching her to ride her bike along the street. She remembered the Halloweens they would walk the neighborhood for candy, and the celebrations during Mardi Gras.

Those were the memories she wanted to hold

on to, not the one of the night her father left.

When she pulled herself out of her memories, she was surprised to discover dark had fully descended. Olivia was going to be worried. Ava turned back to the truck and palmed her cell phone from her back pocket.

She had only gotten three steps and pressed Olivia's name to dial before she was attacked from behind. The phone went flying through the air to land with a *thunk* on the road. A man held her arms at her sides from behind, while another came at her from the front.

Ava kicked out both legs and connected with her frontal attacker. As soon as both feet were on the ground, she threw back her head, slamming it against the attacker behind her. He released her with a savage curse. Ava turned and gave him a sideways kick in the jaw that sent him sprawling to the ground.

She started to run to the truck when two more men rushed her. Every bit of her training in Tae Kwon Do, Ju-jitsu, and Karate were used.

They were trying to grab her, which made it easy for her to block them and deliver swift kicks and punches. It wasn't until they changed tactics and began to hit back that she had to quickly change her own strategy.

She knocked another down, and faced her last two opponents when something slammed into her from behind.

~ ~ ~

"Linc! Damn you. Wake up!"

Lincoln winced and batted at the hands shaking him. "Enough, dammit."

"Then you should've woken up," Christian said, but released him.

Lincoln gingerly sat up. "What the hell happened?"

"Kane, that's what."

Lincoln found his knives and sheathed them once more. "He didn't hurt me."

Christian snorted derisively. "Really? I'd say knocking you on your ass lights out hurt you."

"He didn't attack either of us, little brother. Nor did he rip Paul to shreds. I think that's a good sign."

No sooner had the words left his mouth than the unnatural howl of a werewolf split the air.

Christian's lips thinned. "If he were in his right mind, he'd know better than to do that."

"He's moved on. So should we," Lincoln said as he got to his feet. "Let's get Paul and get going."

Lincoln carried Paul over his shoulder with Christian in the lead with his crossbow.

"Maria's place is closest," Christian said as he turned right instead of left.

Lincoln wasn't about to argue. Paul was heavy, and they still had yet to catch Kane. At this rate, it was only a matter of time before Kane killed someone.

By the time the lights from Maria's house came into view, sweat coated Lincoln and ran down his back and into his eyes. There was no need to call out to Vincent. He would see them soon enough, and come to the house to find out what happened.

Christian let out a bird-like whistle that had Olivia at the porch door in seconds. When she spotted them, she opened the door and motioned them inside before rushing to the house door and flinging it open.

"Is he injured?" she asked.

Christian shook his head. "Just knocked out."

Olivia pointed to the couch and told Lincoln, "Lay him there."

"Where's Maria? Paul could use her herbs when he wakes," Lincoln said.

"She's with Grace," Olivia said. "I called her after Vin stopped by to tell me what was going on with Kane, so she'll stay at Grace's all night."

Christian stood in the doorway of the house. "That's probably for the best. When's the last time you talked to Vin?"

"Hours ago when he told me he'd be out there guarding this area."

Lincoln gratefully accepted the glass of water Olivia handed him as he looked around the house waiting for a glimpse of Ava. It wasn't as if there were many places for her to hide.

"She's not here," Olivia said.

Lincoln jerked his head to her. "What?"

Christian let out a string of curses as he stepped out onto the porch.

Lincoln had thought Ava was safe with Olivia. She should have been. "Why did you let her go?"

Her black eyes narrowed on him. "I didn't

know about Kane until after she left, and that's because none of y'all bothered to tell me until hours later."

Lincoln closed his eyes as he envisioned all sorts of things happening to Ava. She might know about the supernatural and the fact that his family hunted the creatures, but she hadn't been around those beings. And unless there was something he didn't know, she hadn't a clue how to defend herself.

"I've been calling her," Olivia said in a strangled voice.

Lincoln looked up to see her haggard expression for the first time. He felt like an ass for blaming her. "Where did she go?"

"Her old house near Lafayette."

She could be anywhere. Lincoln rubbed the back of his neck. That knot that he felt earlier doubled. He'd known then something was wrong. He shouldn't have ignored his instincts.

"Linc?" Vincent said from the doorway.

Lincoln walked to the kitchen sink and turned on the water. He splashed his face a couple of times before he turned off the water and walked out of the house.

"Linc!" Vincent called.

"I've got to find her. Kane didn't hurt us, but I think he's beyond that now. He'll rip her to shreds."

"Lincoln."

He whirled to face his elder brother. "Don't you dare try and stop me, Vin."

"Be careful."

Lincoln glanced at the ground, all his anger disappearing at the concern in Vin's voice. "I'll do my best."

Christian walked up then. "You find Ava. We'll track Kane."

They were better when they all worked together, but Lincoln knew the need to find Kane was imperative and they couldn't wait for him. "Once I get Ava back here with Olivia, I'll catch up with you."

"A sound plan," Vincent said.

Christian grinned mischievously. "Just don't get your ass knocked out again. I won't be there to wake you."

"Won't be an issue since I don't have to look out for you," he teased in return.

The smiled dropped, because they all knew how quickly life could be taken with what they did.

"Come home to us," Vincent ordered.

It was the same order their mother had given their father whenever he went hunting. "Make sure Beau has something good cooking. I'm already hungry."

"I can come with you," Christian offered.

Lincoln shook his head. "Vin will need both you and Beau to track Kane. Kane is quick and viciously strong. Make sure none of you get bit."

"Ditto," Vincent said. "Having one branch of the family as werewolves is plenty."

Lincoln turned on his heel and walked into the darkness. Ava's life could be on the line, and he'd be damned if he wouldn't be there to find her.

~ ~ ~

Ava woke and immediately grabbed her head. It felt as if a million little men were inside beating on drums. She groaned and sat up. Through the pain of her head she wondered why she felt grass and leaves beneath her hand. Her heart beat a slow, sickening staccato as she looked around to find herself in the middle of a field with Olivia's truck nowhere in sight.

She climbed to her feet and felt the bruises from her fight with the jackasses who had jumped her. But why? Why had they taken her out here?

She looked to her left and saw more open field. To her right was a clump of trees. From the light of the nearly full moon she could make out the cypress trees, which meant she was close to water.

The bayou was beyond those trees. Water moccasins, gators, snapping turtles, and all other kinds of animals awaited her in that direction. But the trees could offer her some protection. More than the open field could.

Ava took a step to the trees, looking around constantly. She had no weapons, nor did she have a cell phone to call Olivia. She was truly on her own, and she was terrified.

She had an awful sense of direction. Not to mention it had been years since she had been in the area, so she had no idea which way to go to find a road or even a house. She could be walking for days if she went the wrong bearing.

Ava let out a sigh when she reached the trees. She leaned upon one and rested her head against the bark. It was going to be the longest night of her life.

The mosquitoes were relentless in their desire to suck her blood. Every rustle of leaves or the sound of the water moving made her jump. Ava had no idea how long she sat at the base of the tree before the bayou went deathly silent. Not even the buzz of a mosquito broke it.

That's when she knew something was out there hunting her, stalking her.

Ava used the tree to get to her feet. Her heart hammered in her chest when she heard a low, rumbling growl that sounded like a wolf.

But she knew there were no wolves in Louisiana. That meant...it was something else entirely.

If she hadn't been so frightened, she would've broke down.

She heard a twig snap to her left. Her head swung around to see something large moving in the shadows.

Suddenly a hand wrapped over her mouth. "Don't move."

Ava about fainted when she heard Lincoln's voice. The relief in knowing she wasn't alone was profound. Then the realization that there was something supernatural out there sent her into a panic.

"Easy," Lincoln whispered near her ear. "That's

my cousin stalking us. I'm not going to let him hurt you, but I also can't kill him."

Ava turned her head to look at him and see if he had completely lost his mind. Their lives were at stake.

"We're going to have to make a run for it," he said as his blue eyes met hers. "Now!"

CHAPTER FIVE

It had been pure luck that Lincoln stumbled across Ava. He was crossing the field when he happened to see something out of the corner of his eye. He had been coming to warn the homeowners when he spotted auburn hair in the moonlight. The terror, the panic that gripped him was indefinable.

He held her hand tight and pulled her after him as they crashed through the bayou.

Lincoln glanced behind him and saw Kane's huge werewolf form gaining ground. They were nothing but bait out in the open, and the only way to stop a werewolf was with silver.

And silver would kill Kane.

There was only one place they could go to be safe. If they could make it in time.

"Faster!" Lincoln shouted as Ava stumbled, but quickly regained her feet.

Her amber eyes were wild with fear. Sweat

made strands of her hair stick to her neck. She clung to his hand with a firm grip. She didn't scream, didn't ask what was after them. She just kept running.

Lincoln kept them out of the water because it would slow them down and allow Kane to catch up. Remaining on land was making them take the long way around as well as draining them of energy.

It had been years since Lincoln had been to the site, and he prayed he remembered exactly where it was. He happened to see a white cross painted on a tree as they ran past, which gave him hope.

"Just a little further, Ava," he urged.

They didn't slow, but Kane increased his speed as if he knew they were about to reach a place he couldn't go. Lincoln withdrew a knife and pushed Ava harder. The site was just a hundred yards ahead, but at the rate in which Kane was gaining on them, they would never make it. Lincoln waited until they got closer before he shoved Ava ahead of him.

"Stay by the oak with the cross!" he shouted.

He turned to confront Kane, only to have a large paw slam into him.

Ava kept running, hoping she would see an oak with a cross on it. She practically ran into it when she tripped over something and reached out to remain upright. That's when she saw the silver cross hanging from a limb, dangling in the middle of the tree where the giant limbs branched out into all different directions.

She turned to find Lincoln and sucked in a breath when she got her first look at what had been chasing them. It was a black furred wolf on steroids. It was easily three times the size of a normal wolf.

Its yellow eyes appeared to see everything, and the sheer size of its paws were astounding, large enough to take off a man's head. But when it lifted its lips and growled, the teeth she saw made her heart miss a beat.

Lincoln was on the ground, and the beast circled. The fact that the wolf was moving kept her focused. Ava took a half step away from the tree.

That small movement drew and focused the wolf's gaze on her. He stared at her as if sizing up his next meal. Ava had never been so frightened in her life, but she had to give Lincoln enough time to get to the tree.

She took another step, and she could have sworn the wolf smiled in anticipation. Her courage was waning fast, and she wasn't sure how much longer she could continue. A quick look at Lincoln showed him watching her with bewilderment. He blinked and looked at the wolf before he rolled toward her a couple of times and then jumped to his feet.

The wolf went nuts at that point, pawing the ground and chomping its jaws furiously as its growls grew deeper and angrier.

Ava rushed to Lincoln and threw her arms

around him. It was only because of him that she was alive. That beast would have torn her to shreds.

"We're safe now," Lincoln whispered, but she noticed he held her just as tight as she held him.

He pulled back and took her face between his hands. He turned her face one way and then the other. "Are you hurt? Did Kane scratch you?"

"No," she whispered, her chest still heaving from the mad dash to the tree.

Lincoln's hands softened and his gaze lowered to her lips. Ava knew she should push him away, but after coming so close to death, she needed to feel something. Which is why she didn't turn away when his head lowered to hers. Lincoln's lips were soft, insistent as he kissed her. His hands delved into her hair, holding her firmly.

But it was the moan that rumbled in his chest that made her shiver with anticipation.

Need burned through her as she stepped closer to him. The kiss deepened while desire flared unchecked. Ava was ready to give in to him – until the wolf snapped its jaws, jerking her out of her haze of desire.

Ava ended the kiss and stepped away from Lincoln. He slowly dropped his hands to his sides but didn't take his eyes from her. While her heart hammered and her body ached for more of his kisses, he stood calm and firm.

It was only the fire in his bright blue eyes that told her he was fighting the passion inside him.

Ava swallowed and looked away. Lincoln might

be hotter than any guy she had ever seen, and his kisses might send her body into overload...but he was a hunter. She refused to go through that again.

"Tell me how a tree with a cross can keep us safe?"

He took a step closer and tilted her chin up with his finger until she was looking at him. "Listen carefully, Ava. We're on holy ground. As long as we remain here, you won't be hurt. Understand?"

She nodded. "That's a big wolf."

"Werewolf," he corrected. He dropped his hands and let out a sigh as he glanced at the creature. "He's also my cousin."

She remembered him saying something about family when they were running, but she was too intent on remaining alive to think much about it at the time. "Family?"

"A branch in New Orleans. They're the LaRues. The first Chiasson that came to Louisiana didn't come alone. He brought his brother. And his sister."

"Ah."

"That's Kane," Lincoln said and pointed to the black werewolf. "A couple hundred years ago the LaRues brought the wrath of a Voodoo priestess upon them. She cursed their family to be werewolves until the end of time."

"They must have really pissed her off."

"I don't even know what they did, truth be told. It's not something they talk about. Even with family."

Ava looked at Kane who was pacing an

invisible barrier from the edge of the water, all the way around the oak, and back to the water again. "Why would Kane travel knowing he would turn?"

"When werewolves turn, they know what's going on. They remember who they are. When the LaRues shift, they make sure to kill deer or cattle. Never humans."

Ava raised a brow. "Want to remind him of that?"

Lincoln walked to the oak and slid down the tree until he was seated on the ground. "That's the thing. It seems my cousin didn't learn anything from his relatives. Kane managed to piss off another priestess. She altered his curse so that when he shifted he would forget that he was human and kill whatever – or whoever – crossed his path."

"He didn't kill you."

"No," Lincoln said thoughtfully. "He didn't."

Ava shivered despite the hot night as she recalled the way the wolf seemed to zero in on her. "He would have killed me."

"Why the hell were you in that field?"

"I was attacked. The men came out of nowhere," she said and wrapped her arms around herself.

"You shouldn't have been alone."

Ave glared at him no matter how his Cajun accent made her blood heat. "I'll have you know it took five of them to take me. I know how to defend myself. I had taken down several before they got the upper hand."

Lincoln's slow smile made her stomach flutter with...was that excitement and pleasure? God, she hoped not. It was already bad enough that she was insanely attracted to him. The last thing she wanted was to seek his approval. On anything.

"Did you get a look at the men?"

"No." And she should have. "They were in all black, and they were intent on taking me no matter what. When I woke, I was in the middle of that field."

Lincoln smoothed down a few strands of hair that had come loose from the queue at the back of his head. "It's pure luck that I saw you at all. Had I went a different route, I wouldn't have."

Ava glanced at the werewolf – Kane – to see him staring at her while he paced. "Where is your vehicle?"

"I was on foot."

"What? Why in the world would you be on foot? It's quicker to go anywhere by car."

"Perhaps," he drawled. "But if I had been in my truck on the road miles from where you were, I wouldn't have spotted you."

"Oh." She found herself looking at the immense paws of the werewolf.

"Besides, I can cross more land on foot if I'm tracking something than I can if I'm in a vehicle."

"Looks as if you found Kane."

"I wasn't tracking him. I was coming for you."

Ava's gaze jerked to his. He had been out looking for her. She couldn't remember the last time someone had thought of her. She had been on her own for so long she had forgotten what it was like to have someone worry about her.

It was uncomfortable to have Lincoln's direct gaze on her. It was as if he knew the turmoil she was in. Ava swallowed and said, "I lost my cell phone. Do you have yours so we can call Olivia or your brothers to come get us?"

"No. We don't carry phones on our hunts. The sound of a ringer or even a vibration could get us killed."

"How are we supposed to get away?" She wouldn't panic. She wouldn't panic.

"We can't."

She was panicking.

Ava turned away, her mind racing with everything that had happened. She needed to put some distance between her and Lincoln.

One moment she was on her feet walking, and the next she saw a blur of black fur and white fangs before she was on her back, Lincoln leaning over her with a murderous expression.

"Are you trying to get yourself killed?" he ground out.

Ava blinked, unsure of what had happened. Then her mind stopped working at all at the feel of Lincoln's weight atop her. Before she could wonder at her body's instant — and traitorous — response, Lincoln jumped off her and grabbed a stick.

Ava sat up and watched him jab the end of the stick in the ground and begin to draw a line. All the while the wolf pawed the dirt and growled.

Lincoln threw down the stick and grabbed her upper arm. He yanked her up and dragged her to the line he had drawn on the ground. "Don't go outside this line unless you want to be Kane's next meal. As you almost were just now."

Ava followed the line to see it made a large square around the live oak about twelve feet on each side. The werewolf stayed just on the other side of the line.

She turned to look at Lincoln. "Thanks for saving me. Again."

He kept his back to her as he stared out over the bayou. Not that she blamed him. She had nearly ended her own life. Not on purpose. It wasn't as if she knew where the barrier was. If she hadn't been so worried about being alone with him, she wouldn't have made such a dumbass move.

Nope. The blame was squarely on her shoulders.

Ava walked to the oak and sat at its base. The night had turned into a nightmare, and she just wanted it to be over.

The problem was, she feared that if she and Lincoln did survive, she wouldn't be able to stay away from him and his sexy, soul-stirring kisses.

CHAPTER SIX

Lincoln thought he had experienced dread before, but that was before he saw Kane lunge for Ava. For a split second, Lincoln feared he wouldn't reach her in time. He still wasn't sure how he had gotten to her before Kane. Yet somehow he had. Lincoln closed his eyes and tried to calm his racing heart.

If something had happened to Ava, it was on his conscience. He was the one who was supposed to keep her safe. The first thing he should have done was mark the ground so she would know how far she could go.

What had he done instead? Kiss her. And what a kiss it had been. He could still taste her, still feel the warmth of her body against his.

He wanted more of her. Needed more of her.

Just as Christian had warned him, Lincoln had to focus on keeping them alive, not on the many ways he wanted to strip away her clothes and make love to her.

Lincoln looked at Kane to find his cousin's yellow werewolf gaze focused with intensity on Ava. If Kane didn't remember who he was, why hadn't he clawed or bitten him when Lincoln had faced him? Why had Kane merely knocked him to the ground and fixated on Ava?

That was twice that night that Kane had let him live. Not that Lincoln was complaining, but it didn't make sense. Something about the entire situation didn't add up, no matter how he tried to look at it.

Lincoln squatted on the balls of his feet and considered their options. With Kane seemingly obsessed with Ava, and with Kane's speed and power, they wouldn't get one foot off holy ground before they were attacked.

Not even the bayous would be safe under a full moon. All animals – supernatural and not – were affected by the full moon. Their only possibility for survival was to remain on holy ground until dawn.

Lincoln looked over his shoulder at Ava to find her asleep. He rushed to her when she began to tilt to the side, getting to her just before she fell. He sat beside her and propped her against his shoulder. She sighed and sagged against him while Kane sat, his gaze still on Ava.

"What are you doing, Kane?"

The werewolf briefly looked at him.

"Why are you after Ava?" Lincoln whispered.

Lincoln looked at the sky. It was going to be

hours before dawn.

~ ~ ~

Olivia paced the floor. She dialed Ava's number again, hoping against hope that her friend would answer this time. Instead of ringing, it went directly to voicemail.

She halted and stared at the phone. If it went directly to voicemail then that meant someone had turned off Ava's phone. And that wasn't good news at all.

Olivia sank onto a chair and closed her eyes. Ava knew what the Chiassons did. She understood the things that were out there. There was no way that she would knowingly put herself in danger.

No matter how Olivia looked at it, it didn't appear good for Ava. But if anyone could find her, she knew Lincoln could. Olivia just prayed that it was before something awful happened.

Lincoln's eyes snapped open when he heard the faint whistle. His brothers had found them. Lincoln let out a sigh of relief and looked at Kane. His cousin hadn't moved. His ears swiveled, indicating that he too heard the noise, but he didn't turn his gaze away from Ava.

"Be careful," Lincoln said into the night to his brothers. "Kane, as we know him, is gone for now."

Kane lifted his snout and sniffed the air. Lincoln could tell he knew others were out there. However, instead of going after them as Lincoln expected, he remained. His brothers wouldn't make any undue noise, which meant no talking. The same didn't apply to Lincoln since he was on holy ground.

"Kane is focused on Ava. He knows you're out there."

Lincoln smiled when he saw a canoe coming toward him in the water. He started to rise when Beau held up his hand. Lincoln frowned. What were his brothers up to?

Beau stopped paddling while he was still in deep water. Kane growled low but didn't go after him.

"We got another call from Solomon," Beau said softly, the water allowing his voice to reach Lincoln.

An uneasy feeling filled Lincoln. "What did he say?"

Beau set the paddle across his lap. "They managed to catch the priestess. With a little...prompting...from Solomon and his brothers, she imparted more information about what she did to Kane."

Lincoln glanced down at Ava. Her deep, even breaths indicated that she was still asleep, and Lincoln had never been more grateful. He looked back at Beau and waited for his brother to continue. The fact that Beau hesitated told Lincoln the news was going to be worse than he had hoped.

"Kane thinks he came here to get away from New Orleans and the threat of killing. He has no idea the priestess sent him."

"For us?" Lincoln asked. "Because he's had two chances to kill me and hasn't."

"No. He was given a target."

Lincoln's heart stopped. He knew exactly who the target was – Ava. But why? As far as he knew, this was Ava's first time back to Louisiana since she left as a teenager. Why would a Voodoo priestess have targeted her?

It was an answer he would find once dawn arrived. He vowed then and there that he would be the one to protect Ava.

"There's more," Beau said.

"How much more can there be?" Lincoln asked. "Kane is after Ava. Do we know why?"

Beau shook his head. "Linc, if Kane kills a human, he'll remain a werewolf forever. Or until he's killed."

The hits just kept coming. Damn. "Did Solomon kill that priestess?" Lincoln asked through clenched teeth.

"They're keeping her alive in the hope that they can...*persuade*...her to lift the curse."

Lincoln blew out a deep breath. "We'll talk to Kane when dawn hits and find out why he was sent after Ava."

"That won't be possible."

Lincoln shook his head. "That bitch couldn't have done anything else."

"She made it so that Kane would remain a

werewolf for the entire cycle of the full moon. He won't shift back to human form at dawn, Linc."

"Then how in the hell am I supposed to get Ava back home?"

"You can't. Kane will follow her through Hell itself if he has to. You have to stay on holy ground." Beau tossed a bag from the canoe onto shore. "Here are some supplies. One of us will be nearby watching. We'll return with more supplies later."

"Ava said she was attacked by five men. See what you can find out about them. I want a chance at the assholes."

Beau's smile was full of wickedness. "Only if I get a go at them as well."

Lincoln gave a nod to his brother and watched as Beau turned the canoe around and paddled away. Anger simmered within Lincoln. If Solomon and the others didn't kill that priestess, he was going to go to New Orleans himself to do it.

He wasn't looking forward to explaining to Ava that they would be spending two more nights – and days – there. Ava was a city girl. She might know how to defend herself, but he didn't see her as the camping type.

Two nights. Alone.

With Ava.

How the hell would he be able to keep his hands off of her? Especially when she used him as a pillow? It was going to be the longest forty-eight hours of his life.

CHAPTER SEVEN

Ava woke to the worst crick in her neck. She grabbed her neck and opened her eyes to see the bayou. Shit on toast. It hadn't been a dream. She really had been attacked by a group of men clad in all black, chased by a werewolf, and...kissed by Lincoln Chiasson.

In that instant, she realized the cushioning for her head was none other than Lincoln himself. Her stomach fluttered at the knowledge that she had spent hours against him.

All those hard muscles.

All that warm skin.

All that sexy goodness.

Ava slowly sat up to find Lincoln looking at her with a grim expression. "What? Did I snore?"

One side of his lips lifted in a half smile. "Only once or twice."

Oh, God. Was he joking? Ava sincerely hoped

so. She stretched her neck and discreetly checked her mouth to make sure she hadn't drooled in her sleep.

The sky was lightening by the minute. Ava couldn't wait to get back to Olivia's to have a hot shower, food, and at least three pots of coffee. She looked to her right where the wolf had been. When she didn't see him, she looked to her left expecting to see the werewolf gone and a man in its place.

Instead she found the black werewolf still staring at her.

"It's dawn," she said, shaken to her core.

Lincoln's chin touched his chest as he sat forward. "My brothers came last night."

"And they didn't help us?" She scooted away from Lincoln, as apprehension iced her veins. "What's going on, Lincoln. I have to know."

"I let you sleep because you were exhausted." He lifted his head while taking a deep breath and met her gaze. "We won't be going anywhere for a few days."

"A few days?" she repeated, wondering how she sounded so calm when her heart pounded against her ribs. Ava searched his face to see if he were joking, but it only took another glance at Kane to comprehend the truth of Lincoln's words. She licked her lips. "What happened?"

"Solomon and the rest of the LaRues caught the priestess in New Orleans. With a bit of LaRue persuasion she told them a bit more about the curse she put on Kane."

It didn't take much for her to guess what it was.

"Instead of reverting back to human form at dawn, I gather the priestess made it so that Kane will stay a werewolf until the full moon cycle is done."

"That's part of it." Lincoln got to his feet and walked to the edge of the bayou within their safe zone. "If Kane kills a human while in werewolf form, he'll remain a werewolf forever."

"That's...a bit extreme. This woman must be a real piece of work."

"Most don't understand that messing with Voodoo is not a good idea. Infuriating a priestess is even worse."

Ava ran her fingers through her hair in an effort to detangle the strands. She gazed at Lincoln's back, wondering what he was thinking, and wishing like hell that she could see his face. "Why do I get the feeling there's more?"

"Did you have any dealings with anyone in New Orleans?"

She considered his words for a minute. "There's a law firm there we were working with, but that's the extent of my association with New Orleans."

"What about your mother?"

Ava chuckled. "My mother doesn't even like to say Louisiana, much less get anywhere near the border. Trust me, she doesn't have anything to do with anyone in New Orleans. Why are you asking?"

Lincoln faced her. The look of regret and frustration caused her stomach to clench in dread. "The priestess sent Kane after you," Lincoln said.

Ava shook her head. "There must be some kind of mistake."

"None. I encountered Kane twice last night, and he didn't harm me either time. Both times he could have. One of my brothers and a friend also had a run in with Kane, and both of them came out of it alive and unhurt as well. I was there when Kane was chasing you last night. He wanted you."

"No."

"Stand up. Walk around," Lincoln urged.

It took Ava a full minute before her legs were steady enough to hold her. She thought Kane was big last night, but in the light of day he was massive. And frightening.

Her gaze was on Kane, and there was no denying the way his eyes narrowed when she stood. He rose up on his paws, the light from the sun soaking into his midnight coat. His lips peeled back to show fangs that were thicker and sharper than she had first thought.

Ava walked toward Lincoln, and Kane was in step with her. When she retraced her steps, he followed.

She was so screwed.

"See how his eyes watch you. See how he looks at nothing but you. Tell me he wasn't sent for you," Lincoln demanded.

"I don't know why he would have been." She began to shake. She had held out hope for dawn, and figured that once the sunlight arrived she could leave the awful night behind and get on with her life.

Lincoln was beside her in an instant. He grabbed her arms and turned her to him. "What about a client?"

"I'm not a prosecutor. I help people like Olivia."

"Then it could be someone you went after while helping a client."

"I suppose. I'd have to look through my files to know for sure."

Lincoln spun around and raked a hand through his hair in frustration. That's when Ava noticed that his hair was down. The long, chocolate strands hung around his face down to his shoulders just begging to be touched.

"There has to be a connection between you and the priestess. She wouldn't have just pulled your name out of thin air," Lincoln said. "And she knew you would be here. How?"

Ava shrugged when he looked at her. "I didn't share my plans with anyone. Not even my co-workers. All they know is that I'm taking some vacation time."

"Olivia said you came on a private jet. Did you have to tell your company where you were headed?"

"I told them it was a short flight. I did have to let the pilots know so the flight plan could be registered."

Lincoln's lips flattened. "That's how the priestess knew. She managed to get them to give her the information."

Ava was happy she hadn't tried to make a move on the co-pilot. "It still doesn't explain why she has focused on me."

"We likely won't know that until we confront her."

Ava lifted her brows at that. "You want to go to New Orleans?"

"Definitely. However, I don't see that happening for a few days. I'd like to know the answers now. Convincing Solomon to bring the priestess here might be more difficult than getting away from Kane."

That reminded Ava that they were stranded for two days. "What are we going to do about food?"

Lincoln pointed to a bag. "Beau brought it last night. They'll return with more food."

Ava shifted feet. "What about...other things?"

A smile flashed before Lincoln turned away. "I'll be on the other side of the oak. It's all the privacy I can give you."

She waited until he had disappeared behind the tree before she went to the water. She knelt beside it and splashed some on her face. It took her two tries before she was able to pull her white shirt over her head to wash up a little more.

The shirt was stained and dirty, but she didn't care about that. It was the way her body ached that concerned her. She looked down at her legs to see the cuts and bruises from her and Lincoln's dash through the woods.

Ava then twisted to try and see her back and right side. She bit her lip when she spotted the edge of a bruise that was already black. It felt like the bruise covered most of her right side.

"What the hell?"

She looked up to find Lincoln staring at her with a mixture of fury and shock. Ava shrugged. "I told you I had a run in with those men."

"How many times did they hit you?"

"Not half as many times as they tried."

He walked to her and squatted beside her. "That looks bad. Where else does it hurt?"

"Back of my head."

She closed her eyes when his hands gently pushed her head down and moved her hair. His touch was light, tender. So at odds with the harsh curse words that tumbled from his lips a second later.

"That bad, huh?" she said as she opened her eyes.

"You've got a pretty big bump. This is where they must have hit you to knock you out."

"That explains the pain." She held her shirt against her chest to hide her breasts. Being around Lincoln made her yearn for him, but it had been years since a man had seen her naked.

His fingers trailed down her spine alluringly, making goose bumps rise over her skin. "Where else?" he whispered.

Ava gathered her shirt higher at her breasts and let him see the left side of her ribs. She hadn't needed to look there to know she would have a bruise. It hurt to breath deeply.

Once more Lincoln's fingers lightly touched her skin. His gaze locked with hers. He was so close she could see the ice blue ring around his eyes.

"Why didn't you tell me last night?" he asked

softly.

"I was being chased by a werewolf."

He smiled seductively. "You are some kind of woman, Ava Ledet."

That kind of compliment coming from a man like Lincoln was high praise indeed. As much as she wanted to kiss him again, she knew it would be a big mistake to get involved with him.

He would always put hunting above anything else. It was in his blood, in his very DNA. She had already been left once. She refused to put herself in that kind of place again.

No matter how much her body burned for him.

Ava turned away before she did something stupid and kissed him again. She stood and turned her back to him while she put her shirt on.

She reached for the bag of food only to look up and see that Lincoln already had it in hand, holding it out to her. When had he stood, much less moved to get the bag? Did he hold supernatural powers as well?

"Eat," he told her. "There's plenty, and more coming."

Ava took the bag and pulled out an apple and a bottle of water. She downed the water first and quickly ate the apple. As she ate, she remembered she hadn't had any food since the day before at lunch. No wonder she felt as if she could eat the entire menu of her favorite Italian restaurant. Twice.

While she munched on a bag of pretzels and a cheese stick, Lincoln found a bag of jerky. She tried not to stare at him, but she couldn't help it. It was only the safety of the holy ground that allowed her mind from going on overload about the werewolf after her. But that gave her mind — and her body — something else to focus on. Lincoln.

How many more times could she find the strength to pull away?

How many more times would she want to?

The fact was, she didn't want to. She wanted to tackle him to the ground and run her hands over his rippling muscles, to feel the strength of him, the power.

If she weren't very, very careful, she would fall into the trap that was Lincoln Chiasson. She would become her mother, waiting every dawn to see if her father would return. Even as a child it had been a horrible existence. How much worse would it be as an adult, and as Lincoln's lover?

Ten times worse? Fifty? A hundred?

She should never have returned to Louisiana. If her father didn't want to be found, then she shouldn't be looking for him. What had it gotten her? Being chased by a werewolf and on the radar of a Voodoo priestess for who knew what reason.

And being attracted to the exact kind of man that she had never wanted to find.

"Why did you pull away?"

She stilled, the water bottle half way to her mouth, and looked at Lincoln. She didn't need to ask what he was talking about, because it was still in her mind. His gaze was on the bayou, giving her the impression that he didn't care about her answer. But he did.

Ava lowered the bottle. "Because I refuse to live like my mother did."

There was a beat of silence before Lincoln's head swiveled to her. "You base everything on what happened to you fourteen years ago? After taking on those five men and holding it together last night while Kane chased us, I didn't take you for a woman frightened of anything."

She was more afraid than he could possibly imagine. Because with Lincoln, she could see herself doing anything just to be in his arms.

CHAPTER EIGHT

The day crawled by, each minute feeling like an eternity. Ava kept her distance from Lincoln, preferring to remain sitting against the oak. Not because she worried he might try to kiss her again, but because she worried *she* would kiss *him*.

She knew when his eyes were on her. Her entire body warmed as if anticipating his touch. As if eagerly awaiting his caress.

And always there was Kane.

The werewolf only took his eyes off of her long enough to get a drink, and then he was back to watching her. Between Lincoln and Kane her nerves were rubbed raw.

The hours of silence also grated on her. It was past noon, and she couldn't go another minute without conversation. She picked at her nails and glanced at Lincoln who walked the perimeter of the holy ground.

"If Kane remains here, then he won't kill a human. That part of the curse will be broken."

Lincoln looked at her as he continued walking. "That's a nice thought, but that's not how a curse from a Voodoo priestess works. If he gets past this full moon, it will happen again, and again, and again, and again. Until the unthinkable happens, and he kills a human."

"Oh." How stupid of her to think there was a bright spot in an otherwise shitty incident.

"I wish you were right. We all do. It's just not how things work."

"My naivety is showing."

Lincoln stopped and tilted his head to the side as he regarded her. "Not naivety. Your optimism, your hopefulness. We...I...forget that sometimes. It's refreshing."

"Perhaps, but without you, I'd be dead, and your cousin would be condemned to a horrible life."

Lincoln turned his blue eyes to Kane. "He wouldn't live long. Between us and his family, he would be put down quickly."

The easy way he said it told Ava that he must have done something similar before. And yet, there was sadness in his gaze. He didn't enjoy what he had to do, but he did it as a necessity to protect those around him.

"Was my father a good hunter?" she asked.

Lincoln grinned as he squatted and picked up a stick that he broke in half. "Not at first, but he was a fast learner. He soaked up every bit of knowledge my father imparted. I remember the first time we took Jack with us on a hunt. He hesitated for only a moment. After that, he never paused again. His aim was always true. He was so good that my father began to take him with us regularly."

"Where did he go, Lincoln? Why would he leave us?"

"I don't believe he did." Lincoln turned his head to her. "Every night before we left the house while my mother was kissing all of us good-bye, he was off in the corner looking at a picture of you and your mother. I don't recall a single time of him actually mentioning your name. He always called you his sweet pea."

Ava smiled at the reminder. "It was his favorite name for me."

"He didn't leave you, Ava. Something happened to him."

All those years of hating her father made tears cloud her eyes. Instead of stroking her hate, she should have been looking for him.

"I wish we'd have known," Lincoln said. "We could've looked for him."

"After all these years, my chances of finding him are pretty slim, aren't they?"

"Yes. I'd like nothing better than to sugar coat things for you, but I won't."

Ava looked at her clenched hands. "I appreciate that."

"I'll help you look when Kane is back in his normal form."

Her gaze lifted to Lincoln. His blue eyes were

clear and locked on her. "You would do that for me?"

"I would do a great many things for you."

The double meaning of his words didn't go unnoticed. Ava shifted under the heat of his gaze. Her body — the treacherous thing — responded instantly.

She might have walked away once, but she wouldn't be able to do it a second time. Lincoln was like a magnet, pulling her toward him, silently urging her to give in. If he knew how precariously she teetered on the edge, he most likely would press his advantage. And part of her wished like hell that he would.

She feared giving in to her desires for him.

But she feared walking away even more.

A whistle broke their focus. Ava was the first to look away. She heard Lincoln sigh as he straightened and turned to the water.

Ava closed her eyes and silently berated herself. Lincoln was a force to be reckoned with, a man who would demand everything of her. He would consume her body, mind, and soul. He would require her love and claim her as his.

She shivered in eagerness.

All the men she knew were metrosexual. None were aggressive or so in control as Lincoln. He was the type of man who would do *anything* to protect his family.

He was the type of man who would give her heaven in his bed.

The type of man who would give unconditional

love.

The type of man who would make the woman he loved his entire world.

She hadn't thought that kind of man existed, except for in movies and books. Yet one stood right in front of her.

Ava looked around him to see a canoe coming toward them. She spotted Christian and jumped to her feet to stand beside Lincoln. Christian smiled at her as he drew closer. His gaze darted to the left where Ava saw Kane out of the corner of her eye. She forced her lips to turn into a smile.

"How are you?" Christian asked her.

Ava nodded. "I'm holding it together."

"She's doing well," Lincoln said. "What did you find out about the men?"

Christian's smile widened. "I'd like to say they'll be waiting for you when this is finished, but Beau and I couldn't seem to stop ourselves. We were giving them a right fine beating when one mumbled something, and all five fell to the ground. Dead."

"Well, shit," Lincoln mumbled.

Ava looked between Christian and Lincoln. "What men? Are you talking about the men who attacked me?"

"Yes," Lincoln said without looking at her. "The priestess made sure to have a plan if they were caught."

Christian nodded grimly. "They took a beating from someone."

"That would be Ava," Lincoln stated.

Ava shifted under Christian's pleased gaze. "I'm impressed," he said.

"She didn't come away unscathed. We need something for her bruises and scrapes, and probably some aspirin for that knot on the back of her head and her ribs."

Christian nodded quickly. "I'll make sure to bring that soon. Olivia packed enough food for a dozen people," he said as he threw another bag at them.

Lincoln grabbed it out of the air and set it down as he opened it. Ava looked back at Christian. "You didn't happen to pack a bed or a TV in there, did you?"

"Not this time," Christian said with a wink. "I'll try to sneak them in the next time."

Ava waved as Christian turned the canoe around and drifted away. How she wished she could be on that boat, but that would be putting so many people in danger because Kane wouldn't stop until he had her.

"Stop thinking about Kane getting you," Lincoln said, breaking into her thoughts.

She looked to find him standing again. "A mind reader, huh?"

"Nope. Just easy to read the emotions on your face. I'll get you out of this, Ava."

"This time. What about the next full moon? Or the one after that? Will I live the rest of my life on holy ground during full moons?"

"We'll find a way to end this."

"Do Voodoo priestesses reverse their curses

often?" she asked skeptically. But she already knew the answer.

"We Chiassons and LaRues can be very convincing."

"It's not just my life. It's everyone else's that gets in the way of Kane killing me. And let's not forget Kane. He didn't ask for this curse, and I'm sure he wouldn't want to be a werewolf forever or have his family hunt him down."

"We'll figure it out," Lincoln said again.

She placed her hand on his jaw, the scrape of whiskers prickling her palm. "Such conviction."

"You act surprised by it."

If he only knew the type of men she worked with. They were good attorneys, but she doubted a single one of them could do what Lincoln did. "I believe you would do everything you could to save both Kane and me, whatever the cost to you."

"I'm willing to pay it."

"I'm not willing to let you. Your family needs you."

He covered her hand with his. "It's not your decision to make."

"I could step off this holy land and end it now."

Lincoln's brow furrowed deeply. "You would do that to yourself and Kane?"

"I'm saying I could. Not that I will."

"So you'd consider ending your own life, but not kissing me again?"

The pain in his eyes was too much for her. Ava threw her arms around his neck and pulled his head down. His lips moved over hers with skill and passion that set her ablaze.

This kiss was intense, savage in the need that pushed both of them. He backed her to the tree and pressed his body against hers. She moaned at the feel of his arousal. He wrapped her hair around his fist and held her head as he plundered her mouth. He robbed her of thought, deprived her of breath.

And she wanted more.

"Tell me you don't want this," he said as he kissed down her neck. "Tell me you don't want me."

"I can't." She clung to him, her body raging with a fire that only Lincoln could put out. "I won't."

He held her head between his hands. Her lids lifted to find his gaze pinning hers. "Try to deny it again, and I'll kiss you until you remember."

"Promise."

Desire flared in his bright blue eyes. "Fuck, yes."

"Stop talking and kiss me," Ava demanded as she yanked his head back down.

No sooner had their lips met than Kane began to growl and snap his huge jaws. Ava had forgotten about Kane and the threat to her life in those few precious moments in Lincoln's arms.

Lincoln chuckled as he backed away from her. "I don't think my dear cousin is at all happy with what we were doing."

Ava looked down at herself to see the sweat and grime. She couldn't let Lincoln have sex with her looking like this. It wasn't just the dirt, she was pretty sure she smelled.

"What did I just promise you?" Lincoln threatened.

Ava motioned at herself with her hands. "Look at me! I'm disgusting. We'll have to wait."

"Wait?" Lincoln asked with a raised brow. "Because of a little dirt."

"I smell."

He threw back his head and laughed. "In case you haven't noticed, I do, too."

"I can't smell you, and you look good covered in sweat." Too damn good, actually. It should be against the law for a man to look that hot while she felt so repulsive.

That seductive grin of his was back. "I look good, huh?"

"You know you do."

"Our lives could end tonight. Do you really want to wait?" he asked as he closed the distance between them again.

Ava pushed his long, dark hair out of his face. "We're not in danger as long as we're on holy ground, right?"

"I'm going to make you pay for reminding me of that," he said as he nipped her ear.

"Promise."

He put her hand on his thick cock. "Fuck yes."

CHAPTER NINE

Lincoln couldn't stop looking at Ava. She had devoured two of the roast beef sandwiches, three snack size bags of chips, a bottle of water and a soda Olivia had packed.

"What?" she asked as she reached for some chocolate chip cookies. "I like to eat."

"I'm not complaining."

"Ah," she said after swallowing a bite. "You're used to the women who eat like birds. That's never been me. I like food. A lot."

Lincoln wasn't sure how he was going to keep his hands off of her for another two nights. She was temptation and enticement, persuasion and fascination. She aroused him to the point of no return only to infuriate him in the next second. She kept him on his toes and in a constant state of arousal.

Ave was a seductress, an enchantress.

A siren.

And he prayed she never left his life.

"Christian's back," she said.

Lincoln looked over his shoulder to see Christian in the canoe, but he had someone else with him. Lincoln jumped to his feet when he recognized Solomon.

"Who is that?" Ava whispered when she came to stand beside him.

"The eldest LaRue, Solomon."

Ava dusted off her hands. "I thought you said it would be difficult to get him here."

"I thought it would be since he also turns during the full moon."

She leaned closer. "Please tell me this Voodoo bitchress hasn't sent another after me."

Lincoln grinned at her. "I doubt it." His grin faded when his gaze met Solomon's. "But it can't be good that he's here."

Kane, who had generally ignored Beau and Christian when they came, began to growl in warning, his fur standing on end as he stared at Solomon.

"He recognizes another werewolf," Lincoln explained.

"Great. I'm all giddy," she said sarcastically.

Solomon looked at Kane with the same blue eyes that Lincoln and his brothers had. That was the only similarity between their families. The LaRues had varying shades of blond hair. Solomon's was a dark blond with strands of brown.

"He looks intimidating," Ava said.

"We hunt in the bayous. They hunt in New Orleans. It's a different beast all together."

Lincoln nodded in greeting to Solomon. "Kane isn't thrilled you're here."

"I'm not happy to be here," Solomon stated flatly. "I had to come. For Kane. And for you."

Lincoln glanced at Christian who merely shrugged in response. It wasn't good news they brought then. Lincoln jerked his head to Ava. "This is Ava Ledet, who your brother is trying to kill."

"Ledet," Solomon repeated.

Lincoln took a step closer to the water. He didn't like the way Solomon was looking at Ava as if she were a morsel he wanted to sample.

"Are you any kin to Jack Ledet?" Solomon asked.

Lincoln held Ava back when she leaned forward. She glanced at him but quickly answered Solomon. "Yes. Do you know him?"

"It all makes sense now," Solomon said more to himself than the rest of them.

Lincoln inhaled deeply and gathered his control. "It might be helpful if you shared it with the rest of us."

"Year's ago Delphine's niece became a vampire and wandered into the parish. Jack killed her."

"Who is Delphine?" Ava asked.

Solomon looked at his brother again. "The Voodoo priestess. She discovered that Jack killed her niece, and she sent her people after him."

Lincoln wrapped an arm around Ava as she

sagged against him. "Delphine had Jack brought to her for revenge, didn't she?"

"Yes," Solomon said.

Lincoln tightened his hold on Ava and asked, "Is Jack still alive?"

Solomon suddenly smiled. "He is. He's been helping us."

"That's where he's been? Locked away by this madwoman and then with you?" Ava asked, her voice breaking with emotion.

Solomon looked at Ava before shifting his eyes to Lincoln. "Delphine is a cunning bitch. She must have learned Jack had a daughter. That's why she used Kane. She isn't finished with her revenge."

"You came all the way here to tell us that?" Lincoln wasn't buying that for an instant.

"I came for Kane. The only one who can go up against him is another werewolf. You need me."

Lincoln knew it was true. Now that they understood why Ava was targeted they could focus on fixing it. "What's the plan?"

Solomon's smile was cold and calculating. "We wait for the moon. I'll...occupy...Kane. Your brothers will get you and Ava to the house."

"Won't Kane still come after me?" Ava asked.

Lincoln faced Ava and turned her to look at him. "Solomon will ensure that Kane is fighting him all night."

"Even if Kane tracks you to the house, he won't be able to get to you," Christian said. "It's also holy ground."

Ava's shoulder relaxed instantly. "And how

soon can we do this?"

"It's not going to be as easy as it sounds," Lincoln warned her. "It's going to take a lot for Kane to be distracted from you. Solomon is putting his own life in danger. He might be a werewolf, but they can still be killed, just like any other supernatural creature."

"I understand," Ava replied.

Lincoln looked at Christian in time to catch a stuffed backpack that was thrown his way. He grunted as he caught the bag and glared at Christian.

His brother merely smiled. "Ava, Olivia packed a change of clothes for you. There is also some aspirin and other things for you."

"What did she pack me?" Lincoln asked.

Christian's smile grew mischievous. "She didn't mention you."

"I'm wounded," Lincoln teased to help lighten the mood for Ava. "I'm going to be her favorite brother-in-law."

Christian rolled his eyes. "As if."

"It's time Vin found someone to carry on the Chiasson name," Solomon said, instantly bringing down the mood.

Lincoln tossed the backpack aside.

"When are you going to take that step?" Christian asked Solomon.

"Not for a long while yet. I'm hoping one of my other brothers does it for me. Women are a hindrance."

Christian shook his head and put his paddle

back in the bayou. "Look for us when the moon rises. Remember, Linc, you're not completely alone out here."

"What did he mean by that?" Ava asked as they watched them drift away.

Lincoln looked around, wondering who was watching them, Vincent or Beau. "My brothers are taking shifts keeping an eye on us, but staying far enough away so they don't draw Kane's attention."

"In other words, we're being watched?" she asked, her eyes wide with mortification.

"We kissed. You could wear that expression if I'd actually taken you as I long to do."

"Is that so?" she asked saucily.

Damn, but Lincoln couldn't wait to get her alone to show her just how she tied him in knots.

And what he proposed to do about it.

Ava was grateful that Olivia packed a pair of cargo pants in the backpack. That, along with the aspirin, the cream for her bruises, and the ponytail holder to get her hair off of her neck had gone a long way to improving her mood.

If the morning had gone slowly, it was nothing compared to the time dragging through the rest of the afternoon. She didn't think the sun would ever set. It was worse than when she was a little kid waiting anxiously for Christmas morning to see what Santa had brought her.

"Will the canoe come on shore? Or will we

need to swim out?" she asked.

He shrugged as he stood with his arms crossed over his chest staring at Kane. "Won't know until they get here and we see how Kane reacts to Solomon."

"Right, right." Was she ever nervous. It was worse than running from Kane that first night. "What happens if Kane doesn't go after Solomon?"

"Then we don't leave."

She hated how calm Lincoln was being. She was being eaten alive by the mosquitoes, and Kane had scared years off of her life.

Ava wished she hadn't eaten that last fig tart. Her nerves were so shaken that her stomach rolled. If she could fight off five men, she could keep her food down.

"My God, will the sun never go down?" she said in exasperation.

"Look at the sunset, Ava."

"I have been."

"No. Really look at it," Lincoln said. He was beside her in an instant, turning her toward the setting sun. "Look at the colors. Tell me if you've ever seen anything so beautiful."

She had to admit the colors were breathtaking. Deep red to orange to pale pink, all with a hint of gold added in. She had been so anxious about the coming night that she had forgotten to enjoy the life in front of her.

Lincoln hadn't though. Was that because there were few nights he wasn't out risking his life?

"I can't remember the last sunset I saw. I'm

normally so busy with work that I don't pay attention."

"Perhaps you work too much."

She snorted. "That's the understatement of the year."

"Do you like your job?"

"I like helping people as I did Olivia. The money is a bonus."

"Do you always see yourself in Dallas?"

Ava knew what he was asking. She couldn't give him the answer he was looking for, but she wasn't sure she could return to Dallas as if nothing had happened either. "It's where my life is."

"Of course."

They watched in silence as the sun dipped below the horizon, and the vibrant colors in the sky faded to gray and then black.

Ava jumped when Kane let out a howl. The full moon shed its bright light upon the ground, and Kane was responding to it. In the distance, another howl sounded. Solomon. Ava wasn't sure she wanted to be anywhere near two werewolves.

"Solomon will know who you are," Lincoln said. "He won't attack you."

"Are you so sure of that?" Ava couldn't shake the way he had stared at her when he discovered who she was. She didn't know why she was more frightened than ever, she just was. "Are you so sure he wouldn't come out here to help his brother kill me if it meant the curse would be lifted from Kane? You would do it for your brothers."

Lincoln started to deny her claim. Then he

closed his mouth and let out a long sigh. "Shit. I hadn't thought of that. He's family."

"And that's his brother," she said and pointed to Kane. "What wouldn't you do for your brothers?"

"There's nothing I wouldn't do for them."

"And Solomon? Don't you think he feels the same way?"

Lincoln ran a hand down his face and turned away to pace a few steps before he faced her once more. "We're taught at an early age that family means everything. We hunt to protect the people of this parish, but family comes first. Solomon was taught the same."

She really hated being right. "We won't know if Solomon is helping Kane or not until I start to go for the canoe."

"Then we don't go. We stay right here."

Ava took his hand. "Do you trust your brothers to help get us to the house?"

"I trust them with my life."

"Then let's give it a go."

"Ava," he began.

She held up a finger to his lips. "You know these bayous, Lincoln. I trust you with my life."

A low growl came from the darkness opposite Kane. Ava watched as Kane's fur stood on end again. Her head swiveled in time to see another wolf, this one silver, step from the shadows.

It had begun.

CHAPTER TEN

Lincoln wanted to call the entire thing off. He was no longer sure of Solomon's intentions. There was a chance Ava would never make it to the house. It was a long way to Chiasson land.

Solomon walked around the oak along the barrier in werewolf form, his silver coat almost glowing in the moonlight. The closer he got, the louder Kane's growls. Solomon's big silver head turned to Lincoln. He met the werewolf's yellow eyes before Solomon issued his own warning growl to Kane.

What would he do for his brothers? Everything. And Lincoln knew damn well Solomon felt the same.

Lincoln took Ava's hand. The tension between Solomon and Kane was escalating at a rapid rate. Any minute now they would begin to fight, and holy ground or not, Lincoln wanted Ava far from them.

There was a flash of light in the darkness over the bayou. Lincoln's gaze jerked to it and found Christian in the canoe hiding behind a crop of cypress trees. Lincoln backed Ava to the edge of the water. They had barely taken two steps when Kane launched himself at Solomon. The growls and general sounds of fighting filled the night like an explosion.

"Go," Lincoln softly urged Ava.

Ava stepped into the water, and Christian paddled furiously to them. To their left another form came out of the shadows. Lincoln let out a sigh when he recognized Vincent. His brother moved to Ava's other side, and the three of them walked deeper into the water.

As soon as Christian was near enough, Lincoln lifted Ava into the canoe and got in behind her at the rear. They both picked up paddles and helped Christian turn the canoe around.

"Hurry," Vin whispered and gave them a push.

The water was like glass, and they glided over it effortlessly. As they rounded the crop of trees, Lincoln looked back to see the wolves still fighting.

"Beau is waiting up ahead," Christian whispered over his shoulder. "Vin will also go around and set up in case Kane gives chase."

"And Solomon."

Christian's silence told Lincoln they too had doubts about Solomon. Lincoln put his energy into getting home. He put his oar in the water and steered them around submerged trees and shallow water while Christian and Ava paddled.

The oars barely made a sound as they sliced through the water. None of them spoke. Until the howl of a wolf cut through the night.

Lincoln set his jaw. If he had to, he would kill both Kane and Solomon. He had vowed to keep Ava safe, and that's what he would do.

A second howl, this one longer and deeper, sounded near them. Solomon and Kane were no longer fighting. The question was, who was closer to them?

"Faster," Christian urged in a whisper.

A shrill cry of pain sounded from one of the wolves. Lincoln paid it little heed. His gaze was ahead of them, looking for the bend in the bayou that would signal Chiasson land. It wasn't that much farther. Just another half mile or so.

The waters of the bayou were deeper in this end. Too deep for a werewolf to try and take them, but there was one place they could. It was called the Bridge, although it wasn't man-made. The waters created it in the bayou long ago. There was a slim area of water between two outcroppings of land where only one canoe could fit.

If even one werewolf were there, it spelled doom for Ava. It was a death trap. Lincoln's only other choice was to pull over and try their luck on land. With as fast as the wolves ran, they stood a better chance on the water.

Thanks to the light of the moon and its reflection off the water, Lincoln spotted the Bridge ahead. The crashing through the brush on either side of them said the weres had caught them. As they drifted closer to the Bridge, Lincoln pulled his oar from the water. Christian did the same and raised his crossbow.

"They're your family," Ava said softly to Christian.

"And they're trying to kill you," he replied.

Lincoln hated how torn he was. He didn't want to kill them, but he refused to allow them to end Ava's life.

Ava shifted to look at him over her shoulder. "You'll never forgive yourself if you kill your family. I'm an outsider here, Lincoln. A nobody. That's your family."

Lincoln's attention was pulled away when he saw Solomon's silver fur out of the corner of his eye. He ground his teeth together when Solomon calmly walked out onto one side of the Bridge and looked across to the other.

"Son of a bitch," Christian murmured angrily.

Ava shook her head at Lincoln. "No."

To the right, Lincoln spotted a dark mass moving through the trees. Kane. He would bunch them in. Which of the LaRue brothers would attack first? Lincoln could already guess their plan. While one attacked and he and Christian fended them off, the other would claim Ava.

It was simple and flawless, especially with the power and size of the wolves.

There was just one tiny catch – they forgot who they were going up against.

Christian caught his gaze and gave him a small

nod. Beau and Vincent were out there, waiting. Lincoln lowered his paddle back into the water to steer them directly at the narrow slit of water.

Ava gripped the oar, her eyes locked on Solomon. Fear kept her muscles tight, preventing her from moving, which was exactly what Lincoln wanted.

The distance to the Bridge grew shorter and shorter. Solomon's large head turned in their direction. Family didn't turn against family. If Solomon and Kane wanted to go after someone the Chiassons were protecting, then all bets were off.

Lincoln and his brothers might not be able to shift into a werewolf, but they weren't lacking in surprises and skill. The LaRues were going to learn a thing or two about them.

They were ten feet from the Bridge when Kane burst through the trees and skidded to a stop on his outcropping. He barked and growled, his huge claws pawing the ground.

Solomon took a step closer to the edge, but paused before he set down his paw. Christian cursed when Solomon took a step back. Lincoln could guess that his brothers had set some kind of trap on either side of the Bridge. Somehow Solomon had sensed it.

Lincoln's adrenaline spiked, his muscles tensed, and his mind focused. He was a hunter. He had saved countless people from the evil that infested the parish. He wasn't about to let Ava down. He reached down and palmed one of his Bowie knives. There was silver in the blade, though it wasn't pure silver. It would be enough to slow the weres down, and give Christian time to get Ava to their land.

Lincoln readied to spring as they came even with the Bridge. Solomon let out a growl right before he leapt over their trap into the air.

Ava screamed, the sound swallowed by Kane's growling. Lincoln dove to cover Ava. Any moment he would feel claws and fangs. Except...there was nothing.

He turned his head to see Solomon had jumped over them and was fighting Kane once again. Lincoln sat back and grabbed his oar that had fallen overboard. "Get moving!"

Christian didn't hesitate. He set down his crossbow in his lap and furiously paddled past the Bridge. Lincoln placed a hand on Ava's back. She was still bent forward, her body shaking. He couldn't wait to hold her in his arms and taste her lips again, but that wouldn't happen until they were on Chiasson land.

He sheathed his knife and joined in paddling them forward. Lincoln glanced back at the wolves just once. It was a vicious fight. He saw blood on Solomon's fur. Whether it was Solomon's or Kane's, Lincoln didn't know.

Another three hundred yards and Christian jumped out of the canoe and pulled it on shore. Lincoln tossed his oar aside and lifted Ava out of the boat. He set her on her feet and turned her to face him.

"You're on holy ground again," he told her.

Her eyes were wide, but she nodded. "I thought

I was going to die."

"And I told you I wasn't going to allow that to happen."

"Ava!" Olivia shouted as she ran from the house.

Lincoln released Ava as Olivia wrapped an arm around her and steered her to the house. He watched them go, amazed that they had made it unscathed.

"Close call," Vin said as he and Beau walked up.

Beau glared at the wolves still fighting. "I want to know how Solomon knew we had a trap set for him."

"It doesn't matter now," Lincoln said as weariness set in. "He kept his word."

Christian nodded. "Agreed. But it isn't over. Solomon will need to get Kane into the cage."

"I'll stay on lookout," Beau said.

Vincent slapped a hand on Lincoln's shoulder as they turned toward the stone building. The building was partially over the bayou on stilts, and was the only part of Chiasson land that wasn't blessed, allowing them to hold supernatural creatures when needed. "Almost done, brother."

Lincoln glanced at the house. He couldn't leave Kane out there to hurt someone, but it was hard not to follow Ava inside the house and just hold her. Never in all his years of helping his family and friends had he ever been so afraid. Afraid that he would fail Ava, afraid that he wouldn't get Ava to safety, but more than anything, he was afraid that she would die.

When they reached the building he walked inside and leaned against a wall before he bent over, his hands braced on his knees.

"Linc?" Christian called.

Lincoln squeezed his eyes closed. "She almost died."

"But she didn't," Vincent said calmly.

Lincoln heard a chain rattle, and knew Vincent was getting the cage ready for Kane's arrival.

"You did everything right," Christian said.

Lincoln straightened and raked his hair out of his sweat-soaked face. "Anything could have gone wrong. I...my God, the fear won't lessen."

"And it never will," Vincent stated.

Lincoln met the gaze of his older brother and realized the truth of his words. "How do you do it?"

"With difficulty."

"Have you ever thought of just letting Olivia go?"

"Many times."

Christian scrunched up his face. "What are you two idjits talking about?"

"Love," Vincent said with a smile.

Christian backed away, lifting his crossbow to rest casually on his shoulder. "Oh, hell no. I want no part of that. I thought Vin had lost his mind, but I understood it because he's always had a thing for Olivia. But you, too, Linc?"

Lincoln threw up his hands in defeat before letting them fall to his sides. "I didn't go looking for it, little brother. She walked into my life, and I had to have her. There was no thinking, just...acting on a driving need, an overwhelming hunger to hold her in my arms."

"You two are bat shit crazy to let women into your lives with what we do," Christian said as he positioned himself at the open door to look out.

Vincent flung wide the sliding cage door. "The Chiasson name must live on."

"Good luck with that," Christian said sardonically.

Lincoln exchanged a look with Vincent before he turned his head to Christian. "Why are you so against falling for a woman?"

"I might not have witnessed Dad finding Mom, but I heard his bellow, heard the anguish and the agony when he found her dead body. I'll spare myself that, thank you very much."

"You don't think you could keep your woman safe?"

Christian snorted. "I think the things we hunt will take us all eventually."

Before Lincoln or Vincent could respond to his remark, they heard Beau's shout from outside. Christian aimed his crossbow through the tall steel doors on rollers.

Lincoln and Vincent used the ladders on the walls to climb on top of the cage. Solomon was the first to burst into the building with Kane right on his heels.

Solomon turned and lunged at Kane. The wolves circled each other until Solomon had Kane positioned in front of one of the cages. He attacked again, backing Kane into the enclosure. When he was fully inside, Lincoln threw the door closed.

The iron and silver mixture of the cage would keep Kane locked away until the full moon had finished its cycle.

Vincent smiled at Lincoln as he snapped the lock in place. Lincoln looked down at Solomon and was surprised to find the eldest LaRue standing next to the second cage.

"You don't have to," Lincoln said.

The silver wolf simply regarded him with yellow eyes. Lincoln jumped to the ground and walked to Solomon. The werewolf was so large he stood almost eye to eye with him.

"Thank you," Lincoln said. "I owe you a debt. Call it in anytime. I'll be there."

"We all will," Vincent said as he joined Lincoln beside Solomon.

Solomon nodded his head in understanding. It was Vincent who opened the cage. Solomon went to the back and lay down on his side.

"We'll be back at dawn," Christian said.

Vincent locked the cage and walked out behind Christian. Lincoln remained for a moment and turned to Kane. The wolf was near rabid in his attempt to get out. It was horrific to watch, and he couldn't imagine what Solomon was going through observing his brother.

Lincoln glanced at the silver wolf. Solomon was watching Kane silently, and most likely would all night. The duties of both families kept them apart, but Lincoln understood the bond of blood. No matter what, Solomon would be there for Kane, just as Lincoln was there for his brothers and Riley.

And Ava.

He turned on his heel and closed and locked the door behind him. Lincoln faced the house and lifted his gaze to the second floor. Ava was waiting.

CHAPTER ELEVEN

Ava showered and got into clean clothes. After all she had been through she should be exhausted, yet she couldn't sit still. She paced the floor of the bedroom waiting for Lincoln. Every creak of the stairs brought her to peek out the door to see if it was him.

She was more nervous than she had been when interviewing at her law firm for a job. She wrung her hands, her mind going over every scene she could think of with Lincoln. She could just come out and tell him she wanted him. Or she could wait for him to make the next move.

Or she could...

Her heart missed a beat when she recognized the sound of his footsteps coming up the stairs. He walked the opposite way of her room, to his. Olivia had made a point of telling Ava where Lincoln's room was.

The sound of his door closing made her jump. Most of her life she had sat on the sidelines or buried herself with studying or work. This trip to Louisiana, back to the beginning, had reset things.

She wasn't the same woman who had gotten off that jet. She thought differently, felt differently. Acted differently.

Lincoln dared her to face her feelings for him. He pushed her to experience the fire between them, and he let loose a raging need for him within her that would never diminish.

Ava refused to wake up the next morning with any more regret. No longer would she push people away and keep them at a distance. She had discovered something precious and rare in the bayous, and she couldn't – *wouldn't* – let it go.

She opened her door and stepped into the hallway. For just a moment, she hesitated. Long enough to square her shoulders. Normally, she would have some kind of plan in place for what she would say, but with Lincoln, she couldn't think straight.

When she reached his door, she heard the water from the shower. Instead of knocking, she tested the handle and found it unlocked. Ava walked inside and quietly shut the door behind her. The bathroom door was ajar, steam rolling out in waves. Her footsteps were quiet on the rugs and wood floors.

Her heart was hammering, but not in fear – in excitement. In anticipation.

In yearning.

She took in the scene of him through the shower doors when she reached the doorway. Ava stopped and smiled while watching the water sluice over his thick muscles and tanned skin. Suddenly his movements stopped, and his head jerked to her. His smile was inviting and daring. Ava pushed down her shorts as he opened the shower door.

She jerked off the rest of her clothes and hurried to him. His large hand closed around her arm to pull her against him. He spun her around and pressed her against the cool tile.

"What took you so long?" he asked.

Ava laughed and wound her arms around his neck. "Close the shower door and kiss me."

"Yes, ma'am," he replied with a wide smile as he reached behind him to close the glass door. "I thought you'd be asking for more."

"Oh, believe me, I want so very much more."

"Really?" he asked and ground his hard cock against her. "How much?"

"Everything you have."

"No more running?"

"No more running."

The conversation ended as he took her mouth in a scorching, searing kiss. Her fingers delved into the long locks of his hair as he deepened the kiss. Her skin sizzled from the heat of the water and the feel of his hard body. She groaned when he slid a hand between them and cupped a breast, stroking his thumb over her already rigid nipple.

Ava clung to him as he kissed down her body before kneeling before her. She looked down at him to see his bright blue eyes filled with desire. She couldn't believe she had found someone like Lincoln, or that she had almost let him go. That wasn't a mistake she was going to make again.

His hands stroked over her stomach and hips before caressing down her legs. He leaned forward and kissed the inside of each thigh. She gasped, her hands slapping against the tile in a futile attempt to remain standing as his tongue licked her sex.

"Lincoln," she whispered in mindless need when his tongue found her clit and began to tease it mercilessly.

Her body was already on fire for him, and it didn't take long to send her to the edge of an orgasm. Without his grip on her hips, she would have been a puddle on the floor.

He licked, he laved. He tantalized, he aroused.

He stirred, he seduced.

Ava was barreling toward her climax when he pulled away. She cried out, needing the release only he could give her.

His body covered hers again. She opened her eyes to see him watching her. The need, the longing she saw in his blue depths made her stomach flip. He wanted to claim her, and Ava wanted to be claimed by him, to have his brand on her so everyone would know that she was his...and he was hers.

As soon as he bent and palmed the back of her thighs, Ava grabbed his shoulders. He lifted her, keeping her legs wide until he was standing straight.

He glanced down and smiled. Then he lowered

her, allowing her back to slide down the tiles. The thick, blunt head of his arousal brushed against her sex. She squeezed her legs in a vain effort to try and wrap them around his hips, but he held her steady.

The feel of him entering her, slowly, caused the breath to lock in her lungs. Ava sank her nails into his skin as he stretched her, whispering her name as he did.

He released her legs so she could wrap them around his waist. The desire was undeniable, the decadence unquestionable.

The pleasure blissful.

She kissed him, letting her hands roam over his back. The feel of his muscles bunching and shifting as he thrust inside her only heightened her senses.

Lincoln couldn't hold her tight enough, could get close enough to her. Need rode him hard, but so did the hunger to imprint himself on her in a way that she could never forget.

Or think of walking away from him.

He thrust deep within her, in time with their kissing. Her tight, slick walls pushed him closer and closer to the edge of oblivion.

No woman had ever wrapped him in such knots before, but it only made him want to keep her by his side. She was smart and stubborn, beautiful and tenacious. She was the woman for him, and he was prepared to do whatever it took to convince her of that.

Lincoln turned them so that the water sloshed her back. She ended the kiss and opened her eyes.

He could drown in her amber eyes.

She leaned her head back to wet her auburn locks as he pumped inside her. The way she tilted her hips sent him deeper, making her moan low and deep. When she straightened, she blinked the water that ran down her face out of her eyes and tightened her legs.

The look of sheer unadulterated need on her face shoved him over the edge. He had been holding on with an ironclad control to prolong her pleasure, but she had destroyed it, shattered it all with just a look.

He pushed her against the wall again and increased his tempo to thrust harder, deeper. Her soft moans turned into cries of pleasure.

Ava could feel the tightening low in her belly, could feel the tension building as Lincoln took her higher and higher. She let herself go, gave up every ounce of herself to him. The look of pure satisfaction in his beautiful blue eyes with his long dark hair slicked to his head was an image she would always hold within her.

The world exploded in a bright light when the orgasm hit. It carried her high, swept her deep. And it mended her broken world.

She was coming down from the high when Lincoln shouted her name and buried his head in her neck. Ava held him tight as he pulled out of her before he climaxed.

For long minutes they remained locked in each other's arms, the hot water cascading on them. When he lifted his head, Ava smiled and wondered how she could have survived another day without Lincoln in her life.

He kissed her softly, gently as he released her legs until she stood before him. Without a word, he grabbed the bar of soap and began to wash his seed from her stomach.

When he finished, Ava took the soap and washed him from head to toe, lingering over the impressive length of his cock. She reached for the shampoo when the soap had been rinsed from his body.

He closed his eyes and smiled contentedly as she washed his hair, allowing her nails to lightly scrape against his scalp. She took her time because the outside world and all the horrors that awaited them were kept at bay while they showered.

All too soon the shampoo was rinsed, and Lincoln shut off the water. He opened the door and grabbed a towel. Instead of handing it to her, he began to dry her himself.

Ava's eyes watered. He cared for her as if she were precious to him. As if she mattered as much as she dreamed she could with someone special.

As soon as he finished with her, Ava stepped out of the shower and found another towel. When she turned back, Lincoln stood outside the shower with his arms out waiting on her.

They shared a laugh. Ava never knew drying someone off could be so much fun. He didn't let her finish. Instead, he lifted her in his arms and carried her to bed.

Beneath the covers, they were once again in

each other's arms. In the silence, she could hear voices below them, but she couldn't make out what they were saying.

"Don't worry. You're safe," Lincoln said.

"Because of you and your family. Thank you."

He kissed her forehead and tightened his arms around her.

"I'm sorry for thinking you had something to do with my father's disappearance. That wasn't fair."

"We were the last to see him. Of course it was fair of you to blame us."

She licked her lips, unable to keep her eyes open another minute. "Do you think he's alive?"

"We'll find out all we can from Solomon. If need be, we'll go to New Orleans."

Now that surprised her. "You would leave your family?"

"For you, yes."

Ava forced her eyes open to look at him. "You're a good man, Lincoln."

"Just don't tell anyone," he replied with a wink.

Lincoln let Ava sleep after their endless hours of making love. They had spent over twenty-four hours locked in his room, coming out only to grab food before closing themselves back in. He wanted to remain in bed with her, but it was past dawn after the last night of the full moon, and he needed to talk to Solomon. Lincoln dressed and quietly left the room.

He hurried downstairs and rounded the corner to walk into the kitchen where he found his brothers sitting at the table.

"'Bout time you showed your face," Christian grumbled.

Beau mumbled something Lincoln couldn't make out and got to his feet.

Vincent shot Lincoln a knowing smile. Lincoln tried to keep from grinning but he couldn't. He punched Vin in the arm as he walked past. The morning sun chased the shadows away. Heavy dew had descended the night before, coating the ground with water.

"Ready?" Christian asked when all four stood on the porch with clothes in hand.

Lincoln was the first to reach the door. He opened it and headed to the stone building, his brothers right behind him.

It was quiet within, and that gave Lincoln pause. He unlocked the sliding door and opened it only wide enough for them to fit through. Vincent clicked on the lights. Kane slept like the dead, but Solomon sat against the metal bars of the cage still staring at his brother.

"It worked," Solomon said. "I had my doubts, but you were right, Vin."

Vincent unlocked his cage. "You can take him home, Solomon. I think Lincoln and Ava will be going with you."

Christian tossed the clothes in to Solomon and checked on Kane's lock. Beau leaned against the wall and used his pocketknife to dig a splinter out of his palm.

Solomon quickly dressed and cut a speculative look at Lincoln. "Bringing Ava to New Orleans isn't a very good idea, cousin."

"Because of this priestess, Delphine?" he asked.

"Exactly. Look what she's done to my family? She wants Ava dead, and she will make sure it's done."

Lincoln fisted his hands. "Over my dead body."

"It might come to that." Solomon shifted his gaze to Christian, then Beau, and finally Vincent. "Is that what the three of you want? To lose your brother to some psycho bitch?"

"No," the replied in unison.

Solomon winced as he pulled the shirt over his head. "I don't want any of your blood on my hands either. Especially not Ava's. I owe her old man. It's because of him that I set some things up before I came here."

"Ah, guys," Beau said as he straightened and looked out the door of the building.

"Right on time," Solomon said with a smile.

Lincoln frowned when Solomon walked out of the cage and past his cousins. They were quick to follow him. Lincoln drew up short when he saw the black Dodge truck. The doors opened, and two men stepped out. One with the blue eyes that signaled him blood, and the second man older, his face more wrinkled and his auburn hair liberally laced with white.

"I'll be damned," Beau said with a wide grin.

"Jack Ledet."

Solomon waved the two men over. Lincoln couldn't take his eyes off Jack. He walked with a slight limp and wore a patch over his left eye.

"That ugly ass walking with Jack is the youngest of us LaRues, Court," Solomon said.

Court rushed Solomon, lowering his shoulder into his gut and tackling him to the ground. The two brothers were laughing when they got to their feet.

Jack didn't stop until he stood in front of Lincoln. "I hear you're the one who saved my Ava."

"It was all of us," Lincoln answered.

Jack held out his hand. When Lincoln had taken it, Jack smiled. "I remember you, Linc. The one who sat quietly sharpening his Bowie knives. Ava couldn't have been in better hands than with you Chiasson boys. Thank you all."

Lincoln started to answer when a flash of auburn caught his gaze. He looked past Jack's shoulder and saw Ava coming toward him wearing jean shorts, a gray tee, and a brilliant smile.

"She thinks you left her," Lincoln hurried to tell Jack. "Be careful with her."

Jack turned to see what had taken Lincoln's interest. Lincoln knew the instant Ava saw Jack. Her smile faded, and she came to a halt.

"Uh, oh," Christian said and disappeared into the woods.

Jack swiped a hand down over his chin. "She's grown into a stunning woman."

"Daddy?" Ava asked.

Lincoln walked around Jack to her. "Solomon had his brother bring your father."

"What do I say?" she whispered, looking past his shoulder to her father

Lincoln tucked her hair behind her ear. "Tell him what's in your heart."

He started to walk off when she grabbed his hand. Her amber eyes beseeched him. "Stay with me."

Lincoln nodded and walked her to her father. Several awkward moments passed with Jack blinking tears away before she threw her arms around his neck. Tears slipped down Jack's face as he held her tight.

CHAPTER TWELVE

"It all worked out," Vincent said and took a long drink of his beer.

Lincoln sat beside him on the porch and watched Ava and Jack down by the shore. They had been talking for hours. "Has it? Ava has her father. There's no need for her to stick around."

"You were going to take her to New Orleans."

"I was hoping that a little more time with me would help her realize..." Shit. He couldn't even say it.

"What?" Vin pressed.

Lincoln shrugged and propped his foot on a post. "That she might care for me."

"Because you love her."

"A person can't fall in love after a few days," Lincoln said derisively.

Vin gave him a droll look. "This coming from a man who did just that, but I think you fell for her the moment you saw her."

"It's impossible."

"Is it?"

Lincoln set down his beer beside the chair. "Ava has a life in Dallas. She's a successful attorney. What could I possibly offer her?"

"Love."

"A life of fear and worry. Christian has it right. Why put ourselves through it?"

Vincent sat up and rested his forearms on his knees. "She hasn't said she's going back to Texas."

"She hasn't said she's staying either."

"Then give her a chance to make that decision." Vin got to his feet. "Besides, when have you ever given up on something you really wanted. If she's worth it, fight for her, Linc."

Worth it? Of course she was worth it. The problem was, Lincoln wasn't sure he was. She had been put through the wringer. What kind of life was that?

She was used to the city, to comfort and fine things. He could protect her from werewolves, but he wouldn't know the first thing about living in the city, wouldn't know how to be the kind of man she was used to being around.

Fight for her?

He would die for her a thousand times over.

Ava looked all over the house for Lincoln. It was Beau who finally told her he was in the building with Kane. Not even that stopped her from going to him.

She walked inside and found him near the far wall next to Kane's cage, leaning back in a chair and balancing on the two back legs.

"I've been looking for you," she said and glanced at Kane who was still laying on his side, asleep, his back to her in human form.

"How did the talk with your father go?" Lincoln asked.

"Difficult at first, but then better," she said as she stuffed her hands into her front pockets. "He killed Delphine's niece outside our house. She was trying to get in my window. He took the body away to dispose of it, and that's when Delphine's people caught him. They took him to New Orleans where she held him for years."

Lincoln lowered the chair to the floor. "Is that how he lost his eye?"

"Yes. She wanted to kill us, but he wouldn't tell her anything about Mom or me. By the time her people came looking for us, we were gone."

"She found you anyway."

"That was because of me. I sent a private investigator looking for my dad. Apparently, the PI went to New Orleans, and his questions caught Delphine's attention."

Lincoln stood and walked to her. "How did Jack get free of Delphine?"

"Your cousins. They healed him, and he chose to remain with them so he wouldn't lead Delphine to us."

"What happens now?"

So that was why he was acting so weird. He thought she was leaving, and perhaps for a while even she had thought that. Until she realized what type of man she would be letting get away.

"That depends," she answered.

He kicked at the leg of the chair. "On what?"

"You."

His gaze lifted to her face. "What about me?"

"If you want me."

The last word hadn't left her mouth before she was against his hard body, his face inches from hers. "Want you? You fool, woman. I'm pretty sure I love you."

She couldn't form a coherent word. She had held out hope that he wanted her to stay. It never occurred to her that he might love her.

"Say something," he said and gave her a little shake.

The only thing she could think of was to throw his words back at him. "Took you long enough."

He smiled and lowered his head. Just before his lips touched hers he said, "Stay, Ava. Stay for me, for us. I'll love you from now until eternity."

The kiss was toe-curling, reminding her of just one of the many reasons she couldn't walk away from him. When he ended the kiss, she drew in a shaky breath and smoothed his long hair away from his face. "I'll stay for you, for us, because I love you too, Lincoln Chiasson."

EPILOGUE

One month later...

Ava looked around her new office with approval. She had always wanted to start her own practice, and by deciding to remain in Louisiana, it had given her that opportunity.

"Mighty fine digs," Beau said as he and Lincoln finished hanging the last of the pictures.

Ava beamed. "I can't believe I officially open tomorrow."

Christian adjusted the filing cabinet next to the reception area. "Can you really say that after already taking on three clients?"

She shrugged. "It's not as if I could turn them away before I had the office up and running."

"That's my girl," Lincoln said with pride in his voice.

Olivia walked through the front door with a

box of files from the law firm. "These came from Texas. I'll get to work on them tomorrow."

"You have more experience than required to be my receptionist," Ava said.

Olivia gratefully handed the box to Beau who sat it on the front desk. "You need help, and I need a job. Seems a perfect solution."

Lincoln walked over to her and wrapped an arm around Ava's shoulders. "You two spend so much time together already while planning the wedding."

Olivia cut her eyes to him. "I needed help. Since y'all are so adamant about keeping Riley in Texas, of course I turned to Ava."

Ava winked at Olivia. "We might need to take a trip to Austin and pay Riley a visit. I'd love to meet her."

"She'll love you," Lincoln said, though his forehead was furrowed. "But if you go, she'll want to come back with you."

"This is her home," Ava stated. "I tried to stay away, but I eventually returned. So will Riley."

"The hell she will. If I have to go to Austin and find her a husband, she won't be coming back," Christian declared.

Ava and Olivia exchanged a look, deciding it might not do the Chiasson boys good to know about the phone call they received from Riley just the day before. Everyone needed a surprise every now and again.

Look for the next Chiasson story –
WILD NEED – Coming August 2014!

Until then, read on for the sneak peek at **FIRE
RISING**, the second book in the Dark King
series…

Dreagan Industries

"Who is that?" Tristan asked.

Laith watched them a few more seconds before
he said, "I gather by the way Jane is fussing that
she's Sammi, Jane's half-sister."

While Banan took Duke's collar, Jane ushered
Sammi into the house. Just before Sammi walked
in, her head turned and she looked right at Tristan
with her powder-blue eyes. It was like a punch in
the gut.

Startling, disconcerting.

Amazing.

The surprising connection that seemed to zip
between them left him pitching, tumbling.
Plunging.

And he wanted more. So very much more.

"Tristan?"

He pulled his gaze away from the now-empty
doorway and looked at Laith. "What?"

"Whatever you're thinking involving Sammi, I
wouldna advise it."

Tristan frowned and glanced at the house,

wondering what kind of injury Sammi had. "What do you mean?"

"Forget it." Laith gave a shake of his head, a wry smile upon his lips. "I've got to see what happens next. Come on. Let's go meet Sammi."

The fact that Tristan wanted a closer look at the woman should have been enough to make him walk the other way. He was just getting ensconced in his life at Dreagan. Phelan and the other Warriors were complicating things enough. Tristan certainly didn't need a woman added to the mix.

Yet he followed Laith into the manor. The sound of voices came from the kitchen. As they stopped at the doorway of the kitchen they saw Elena pouring some tea and Jane fixing a sandwich while Sammi sat at the table desperately trying to stay awake.

He found his gaze drawn to her no matter how hard he tried to look away. Even in profile, she was beautiful with her long, graceful neck and her fall of sandy-colored hair about her. She sat tall and straight in the chair, as if it was as natural as breathing.

Tristan saw her fall asleep twice and jerk awake both times. The third time, she listed to the right. He rushed to her, grabbing her just before she hit the floor. Jane, Elena, and Banan turned as one from whatever they were doing to gawk at him.

He gazed down at the woman who slept in his arms, completely taken unawares as he looked into her oval face. Her cheekbones were incredibly high, her nose small, and her lips as decadent as sin.

Even in sleep, she made his body hunger to know her, his lips crave to taste her, and his hands ache to caress her. Desire shot through him like lightning, making him burn.

Making him yearn.

Tristan moved a strand of her hair out of her lashes and wished she would open her eyes so he could look into their cool color once more.

Then he remembered where he was, and just who he was holding. "I think the food is going to have to wait."

"I knew she looked tired," Jane said, a frown marring her forehead.

Tristan easily shifted Sammi's body into his arms and stood. "She's too skinny."

"I knew she had lost weight too," Jane said with a shake of her head. Then she looked at Banan. "I think she's in some real trouble."

"We'll get it out of her," Banan promised.

Tristan was careful not to touch Sammi's left arm as more blood seeped through her shirt. "What about her injury?"

Banan let out a string of curses as he walked from the kitchen. "She said it was nothing. Bring her, Tristan."

Jane was at his heels, tripping twice, as he followed Banan up the stairs. Despite both of them watching him like hawks, Tristan found his gaze drawn again and again to the woman in his arms.

Her hair, a unique mixture of blond and light brown, hung over his arm, the waves teasing him to touch them. Her exhaustion and injury worried him that someone had pushed her to her limits, and he wanted to know who had done that to her. And why.

Thank you for reading **Wild Dream**. I hope you enjoyed it! If you liked this book – or any of my other releases – please consider rating the book at the online retailer of your choice. Your ratings and reviews help other readers find new favorites, and of course there is no better or more appreciated support for an author than word of mouth recommendations from happy readers. Thanks again for your interest in my books!

Donna Grant

www.DonnaGrant.com

ABOUT THE AUTHOR

New York Times and *USA Today* bestselling author Donna Grant has been praised for her "totally addictive" and "unique and sensual" stories. She's written more than thirty novels spanning multiple genres of romance including the bestselling Dark King series featuring immortal Highlander shape shifting dragons who are daring, untamed, and seductive. She lives with her husband, two children, a dog, and four cats in Texas.

Find Donna Grant online at:

www.DonnaGrant.com

www.facebook.com/AuthorDonnaGrant

www.twitter.com/donna_grant

www.goodreads.com/donna_grant

Never miss a new book
From Donna Grant!

Sign up for Donna's email newsletter at
www.DonnaGrant.com

**Be the first to get notified of new releases and
be eligible for special subscribers-only exclusive
content and giveaways. Sign up today!**

CPSIA information can be obtained at www.ICGtesting.com
Printed in the USA
LVOW11s1555030614

388428LV00006B/838/P